CAMP DAVID HAS FALLEN!

CODY'S WAR BOOK TWO

STEPHEN MERTZ

**WOLFPACK
PUBLISHING**
— EST 2013 —

Paperback Edition

Copyright © 2019 Stephen Mertz

Published in the United States by Wolfpack Publishing, Las Vegas

Wolfpack Publishing
6032 Wheat Penny Avenue
Las Vegas, NV 89122

wolfpackpublishing.com

Paperback ISBN 978-1-64119-659-8
eBook ISBN 978-1-64119-658-1

Library of Congress Control Number: 2019952810

CAMP DAVID HAS FALLEN!

CHAPTER 1

A frigid February breeze knifed in off the Atlantic.

Jack Cody spared a glance down at the pavement twenty-eight floors below. He was cat-footing his way along the rain slick parapet of the Grand Ocean Towers. Far below, pre-dawn traffic crisscrossed like fire ants in a busy hive.

How easy it would be, he thought. A simple misstep and plunge to his death. . .

"Hey, Jack," the voice of Sara Durell resounded through the earbud, *"you awake?"*

The moment passed and Cody shook it off—too easy. When death took him, he wanted to go knowing he'd *earned* it.

Cody was a big man, muscular and well-proportioned in black combat fatigues from which dangled implements of violence.

"I'm awake," he responded to his control officer via their comm link. "Going dark," he added.

He established radio silence between them with a tap of his thumb before she could voice protest. He gained the target point. He crouched, removing the thirty-meter climbing single rope from a satchel at his side. He withdrew a four-tine grappler, tied it to a stanchion and doubled up to slide the rope through a carabiner. He tested his weight. Then he vaulted off the side without hesitation to the wide balcony of the suite below.

Despite his size, the neoprene soles of Cody's combat boots muffled his drop to the deck. Cody tied off the rope to the concrete-and-steel balcony railing. He side-stepped to where the corner met the sliding glass door. The opposing door stood wide open—the night wind swirled the sheer curtain to and fro. Perfect sleeping weather in Fort Lauderdale this time of year. He whisked a Beretta M9A3 pistol from shoulder leather and eased along the sliding doors until he could peer into the room.

A pair of nude bodies lay intertwined, backs to Cody, the male with his arm draped over his companion. A night-light from the bathroom provided the only beacon to pierce the gloom.

It would have been easy to kill the guy in his sleep—a half-dozen techniques ran through Cody's mind, all of them quiet, tried and tested many times before. But he wasn't here to kill. At least not unless absolutely necessary. This time it was strictly a search-and-rescue mission. Cody clamped a vise-like grip over the young man's mouth and nose. It jarred the young man awake but with all airways obstructed he couldn't cry out.

Cody pressed the cold barrel of the pistol to the man's temple. He whispered, "Not a word."

Maintaining his hold, Cody practically dragged the kid from the bed and onto his feet. He released his nose and mouth but kept the advantage with his forearm locked against the young man's chest.

"Name."

"M-Mason."

"Mason what?"

"Narmy, Mason Narmy."

"How old are you Mason Narmy?"

"Twenty-three."

"Want to see twenty-four?"

The young man returned a herky-jerky nod.

"Find your clothes and get dressed."

Mason scrambled to do as instructed while Cody rummaged to find the switch to a wall light mounted near the bed. He clicked it on, then grabbed the comforter and tossed it across the bed to cover the nude form of the young woman he recognized. Shayna Harwood stirred in her sleep, then raised her head, squinted against the light, and looked at her companion.

"What are you doing?" she mumbled, her sleep-addled brain not yet processing the third figure in the room.

Mason didn't answer her but instead hopped around trying to stab one leg into the tight designer denims.

She repeated her question and then must have spotted

Cody in her peripheral vision, because she turned to glance at the specter-like figure. Naturally, her eyes grew wide. Cody didn't act surprised, expectant she would react much the way she had.

"You," she said. "You have some explaining to do."

Cody's eyebrow arched and he felt an involuntary quirk at the right side of his mouth. "Oh no, my dear. *I* don't have any explaining to do."

Shayna sat suddenly, oblivious to the blanket that slid to reveal a young, perky breast. "What's the idea of busting in here and scaring us half to death?"

Cody crossed to the bed and readjusted the blanket. "Get up, go to the bathroom, get dressed. You're coming with me." He spared Narmy a glance and added, "*Both* of you."

"I'm not going anywhere. I'm a full-grown adult and a daughter of the President of the United States."

"Shh!" Cody put a finger to his lips. "There's no reason to announce it to the whole floor, Shayna. Now get dressed. Please."

Shayna stared holes through Cody before she jumped to her feet with blanket dragging behind her, making no attempt to cover her backside. She stormed into the suite-style bathroom and slammed the door.

Narmy finally had his jeans zipped and was popping into his t-shirt as he asked, "How the hell did you find us?"

"Not hard if you know what to look for, kid."

"I'm no kid."

Cody smiled. "Yes, you are."

Narmy sized him up. It wouldn't have been any contest. Cody stood well over six feet. Dark wavy hair with stark white streaks at the temples implied his life experience. Narmy couldn't have been an inch over five-foot-ten and had the physique of a ballet dancer. All show muscle.

"We're consenting adults, you know."

"Not having this argument." Cody stashed his pistol. "I'm in no mood. You can take it up with her father."

"What if I don't want to leave?"

Cody's smile was pure frost. "I throw you over one shoulder, Shayna over the other, and off we go on a merry adventure."

Shayna emerged from the bathroom, and Cody mused he'd never known any woman who could dress that fast. She had the dark eyes of her mother and they burned with fire at the moment. Deep down it probably wasn't much of a surprise to her. She'd known Cody for years—so did all of POTUS's immediately family for that matter—so she could act shocked, but it was just that: an act.

"There's going to be hell to pay for this," she announced.

No argument there, Cody thought.

Something began to gnaw at his gut and Cody felt the hairs on his neck stand straight. His sixth sense had kicked in and coupled with the sound of harried footsteps sidling up to the hotel door. Fate had just introduced a new group of actors to this drama. By the fact the group outside of the door had made noise by trying to be quiet, their unfriendly intent seemed obvious.

"That hell will have to wait," Cody said, gesturing them toward the door. "A new kind's arrived. Both of you to the balcony. Now."

"And do *what?*" Shayna demanded, hands on hips.

"You'll know when you see it." Cody looked at Narmy. "Now take her and go."

✳✳✳

Sara Durell watched the infrared signatures of a half-dozen armed men approach the hotel room.

The grainy images displayed on the IR system aboard the Airbus H145 helicopter weren't the highest quality given the distance, but they were adequate enough to paint the picture. Per SOP, they had gone to radio silence once Cody actually reached the original target. He wouldn't want her to break protocol and ordinarily Sara wouldn't have done so, but this was a bit of a special situation in her mind: she wanted Jack to come out of this alive—regardless of his personal sentiments.

"Jack, you have at least six, say again *six* targets nearly on top of your position."

"Let me guess," he replied quietly. "They're outside the door."

"Roger that."

"Already heard them approach. It must be amateur hour."

Okay? Sara thought. "But why would anyone–"

"Angel One and her beau are on their way to the roof. Good chance we're going to need a fast exit."

"No safe place for us to land there," Sara said.

"Who said anything about landing?" Cody countered.

Sara shot a querulous glance to the man in the pilot's seat next to her. "Please tell me he's not suggesting what I *think* he's suggesting."

Owen McConnell sighed as he stabbed several switches above his head to begin preflight checks and warm-up. "Okay, I'll tell you he's not suggesting we hover above the hotel and use the rescue winch to haul them up."

"That's crazy! There's very little margin for error on the rooftop of the Grand Ocean Towers. That's why we couldn't land there to begin with."

McConnell flashed her a wicked grin as the five-bladed turbine rotor began to move. "Don't worry, my dear. I can hold her in place."

The pilot's abilities were the last thing Sara worried about. Colonel Owen McConnell, affectionately known as "Blades", had served as a veteran pilot of three wars, and currently held the right seat aboard Marine One. He'd also been a personal friend of POTUS for more than two decades and bore the distinction of being one of the most decorated pilots in the history of the U.S. Marines.

Sara disengaged her seat belt. "Guess I'd best get back to that winch."

✳✳✳

Cody extinguished every light in the room before double

checking the action on his M9A3. He took a position behind the wall where it met the hall. This gave him a clear view of the hotel room door.

He'd brought only the one firearm on this retrieval mission, not expecting Shayna's lone company to offer any sort of resistance. Cody had definitely *not* expected to run into the kind of trouble now looming outside the door. But that also meant they weren't expecting him either and, he planned to use that to his tactical advantage.

The door didn't swing inward with violent force. Cody detected a muffled beep and heard the click of the lock disengage before light from the outside hall spilled gradually from the ever-widening gap. Cody crouched to provide minimal exposure, pistol held ready, and braced his left hand against the wall.

Two figures emerged from the exposed doorway—one coming in high, one low—as they tracked the area in front of them with the muzzles of their weapons. Even in Fort Lauderdale, the cops didn't tend to carry SMGs, and U.S. military special operators utilized either H&K MP7s or M4 CQBRs.

Confident these were non-friendlies, Cody squeezed the trigger twice on the intruder who'd come in low. A pair of 9mm Parabellums drilled through the man's chest and drove him into the legs of his partner, causing the latter to stumble.

Cody fired again, this time sending a third round through the second man before he could fully recover his balance. The man's body bounced off the door frame in a queer fashion and he toppled backward into the hallway.

It didn't become immediately apparently to two more combatants just outside the doorway the exact origin of the shots, but they got wise enough to get clear before Cody could tag another one. Clearly, they hadn't expected someone to bring the fight to them, rather relying on their numbers and superior firepower as sufficient to make their mission a cakewalk.

The delay gave Cody just a heartbeat moment to get clear before the remaining four men in the hallway sprayed the interior of the hotel room with bullets by exposing only the muzzles of their weapons. By the time they'd expended their magazines, Cody had gained enough time to get on the balcony and see Narmy climb over the parapet before he disappeared from view.

Cody gave a nod as he holstered his pistol, spit into his hands, and then grabbed hold of the rope and began his ascent. He felt naked as he climbed with his back to the enemy. They could come out to the balcony at any moment and shoot him while he was helpless to defend himself. He couldn't bear the thought of going out that way. No glory.

When he was about three-quarters of the way, Cody wrapped his right hand around the rope to stabilize his position. Left hand now free, he reached to his belt and withdrew the only other offensive tool he'd brought with the idea it might come in handy. The M84 stun grenade was hardly lethal but it could provide enough distraction to capture an enemy.

Or evade one.

Filled with a pyrotechnic mix of magnesium and ammonium nitrate, and capable of a five-foot blast radius, it would be perfectly safe to deploy on a hotel balcony without risking structural or collateral bystander damage. Cody stuck his thumb through the pin handle, pulled it clear, and dropped the grenade to the balcony below. He resumed his climb and reached the parapet a couple of seconds later just as the grenade blew with a 180-decibel report and an eight million candela flash.

Cody completed his climb and rolled over the parapet to land on his back. He laid there a minute. Finally, after catching his breath, he engaged his throat microphone. "Ready for extraction."

"If you'd bother to look up you can see we're already here," Sara's voice resounded. "So quit your loafing. This ain't Uber."

That's when the whipping of the wind against his face and steady chop of rotors brought Cody back to the here and now.

CHAPTER 2

All aboard as the MilSpec-equipped chopper disguised to look like a civilian commercial charter buzzed across the skies of Fort Lauderdale, Cody took a moment to study the rescued. For a time, he exchanged glances with the couple, pinned them with an icy stare.

What could he say?

A lecture wasn't appropriate under the circumstances—maybe it would have been properly parental but unaccepted coming from him—since these two were allegedly consenting adults, despite the fact they hadn't acted like it. But there wouldn't be another chance and to Cody's way of thinking, while they didn't have to heed his advice, they were prisoners to at least hear him.

"Stupid," he finally said through the back-channel headsets they all wore. "In a word, stupid."

"Says you," Narmy shot back

Cody nodded with a hardened look. "Yeah, says me, and

I think I know just a little bit more about it than you, junior. This little stunt you pulled resulted in loss of life for other human beings."

"Bad men," Shayna said.

"Maybe," Sara interjected, glancing to the trio from the jump seat. "The plain fact of the matter is we don't know *who* they were. Which is a different matter entirely we'll have to investigate."

"I don't know who they were," Shayna said matter-of-factly.

Narmy added, "We were checked in under assumed names. I even had IDs made."

Cody noticed Sara's eyes twinkle in the amber lights of the cabin. "Is that right? Well, obviously you didn't do a good job. And if they still knew who you were even under a false identity it would seem to point to the fact they may have been after *you*, Mister Narmy."

"I don't—"

"No," Cody said. "Your only job right now is to shut up and answer questions."

"Who were they?" Sara asked.

Narmy looked uncharacteristically sheepish.

"I'm…I'm not sure. They could be…"

"Quit stuttering and speak up!"

Sara interjected more quietly, "Jack. It might have something to do with his work." She returned her gaze, softened some, to Narmy. "You're Mason Narmy. Twenty-three years of age, a junior cryptanalyst with the NSA."

Narmy maintained a poker face. "How did you know?"

"It's our business to know," Cody said. "So, we can pull you out of scrapes like tonight you don't even know you're in."

Sara continued. "The men who were in that hotel were professionals. Armed with automatic weapons. They were on a mission and they knew where to look. They weren't cops or DEA, so that rules out warrants or a drug raid. They very specifically selected that room, and I highly doubt they had any reason to be looking for Shayna."

"That's a lot of guessing," Narmy replied.

"Not my habit to guess. The situation happens to fit the facts as we know them. There's a pretty good chance, since you were using false IDs, they probably had their hooks into the camera system or hotel reservations. Since 9/11, many hotels now scan actual identification that includes an encoding of the info plus the photo. Whatever the case, you likely tripped a face recognition bot. Did you both show ID?"

Narmy shook his head. "Only me. I booked in as alone."

"Since Shayna is highly recognizable, all the more likely *you* were the one they had under scrutiny then," Sara said.

"In any event, they were gunning for you," Cody observed. "Maybe they were there to kill you, maybe just take you hostage. The big question is why."

"And more importantly," Sara added, "is it possible they still have you under observation?"

Cody glanced at her. "We can't take them together. Safer to split them up."

Sara nodded as she switched over to the pilot channel. "Agreed. Owen, we need to make a detour. Please arrange a flight to Andrews."

***

It was hitting midday as the charter jet entered the private hangar at Andrews Air Force Base. It hadn't taken any time to get all the proper clearances—Blades McConnell had connections in practically every part of the world, which was doubly useful when Cody needed to get someplace fast. In this case, his credentials and clearance as pilot of Marine One were more than enough to get him a priority flight plan and touchdown.

Cody lowered the ramp and tossed his duffel onto the hangar pavement before squeezing his big frame through and descending the steps.

He turned to help Shayna out next, followed by Narmy, and finally Sara.

"Say your goodbyes, Shayna," Cody said. "You have five minutes."

Cody didn't wait for a reply as he shouldered the duffel and turned, somewhat in a brooding mood now, and headed toward the office to find a cup of coffee. Sara was on his heels, rushing to match pace with Cody's long strides.

"Damn it, Cody," she finally managed. "Slow the hell down!"

He stopped to face her. "What?"

She made a search of his eyes. "What's going on with you?"

"Nothing. I'm just not keen on being a babysitter. I don't have time for that when there's bigger missions I could be doing. Plus, I'd rather go out of this world in a terrorist explosion than die from extreme heights trying to rescue two adults acting like kids stealing a first kiss behind the shed."

"You saved their lives."

"Not the point." Cody turned and continued for the office.

"Will you *wait* a minute, please?"

"I can listen while I walk."

"I reached POTUS. He wanted me to thank you and asked if you would do one last favor."

They passed through the door into the office and Cody spied the coffee machine immediately. The room was broken into two sections, one with a couple of round tables and metal folding chairs while the other had a couple desks with computers and phones. Cody dropped the duffel on one of the tables and headed to the coffee machine.

"What does he want now?"

"He wants you to go to Camp David. Me, too. And he wants us to bring Shayna there."

Cody poured his coffee. "You can do it. She's pretty secure now, I don't think this requires me."

As Cody took a first sip, Sara said, "It wasn't a request, Jack."

Cody screwed his face and smacked his lips. "This stuff tastes like dirt." He looked at her. "Did he use favor and request in the same sentence?"

"What?"

"You said he asked another favor but then you said it wasn't a request."

She sighed. "Okay, well consider it a favor to me."

"What does he really want, Sara?"

"Okay, fair enough. He didn't say it directly, but I think he wants to thank you personally. And I think he wants to pin a medal on you."

Cody shook his head. "Nope. Don't need it, don't want it."

"So, you won't do this even for me?"

Cody took another sip and mused it tasted better now. As he took a seat at the table he smiled at Sara. "Maybe it wasn't the coffee after all. Might be just his request left a bad taste in my mouth."

Sara sat across from him. "Jack, sometimes you're a subversive sonofabitch. I know you very well and I know why you don't want to do this. But what you do is important, no matter how much you may not think it is."

"What do you want from me, huh?" Cody shook his head. "I have no time to go prancing myself in front of POTUS so he can shower me with gratitude. I did my job. His daughter is safe. That should be enough."

Sara arched an eyebrow and gave him "the look".

"Let me remind you that I keep your schedule and I've seen it for the next twenty-four hours. You're not busy." Then she smiled.

Cody knew the futility of arguing with her, but they had to do this—it was part of their very complex relationship and they bickered honestly like good friends were wont to do. So, he nodded in assent.

She smiled. "That's better. Besides, lots of open ground there. You could go for a long hike or maybe take a hunting rifle and shoot some rabbits—he invited you to stay a few days. I promise I will do everything I can to suggest POTUS keep the ceremony short, sweet and private."

"Oh...swell."

It was officially known as the Naval Support Facility Thurmont to the military, but the rest of the world called it Camp David. Thus named by President Dwight D. Eisenhower in honor of his father and son, other Presidents had given it its own monikers. FDR had called it Shangri-La and its original name had been Hi-Catoctin after its location near Catoctin Mountain Park.

Regardless, President Martin Harwood liked it for its isolated location and the security.

Staffed by mostly Navy and Marine Corps personnel, the place was nearly inhospitable during the Maryland winters. That made it perfect for the president's purposes on this occasion. The rest of the first family would arrive in a few hours, but at this point and time Harwood expected another guest in short order.

Not a member of the first family or even an American, but no less important.

As if someone had been reading his thoughts as he sat at the desk of his presidential office in a wing of the main cabin, an office adjoined by a fully equipped high tech briefing room, Jim Corbett rapped on the door.

"Sir, he's here."

Harwood nodded and gestured for them to escort the guest

as he took a quick glance in the small mirror on his desk. A naturally round face of which there was more than there once had been peered back at him. Well, at least he still had some salt-and-pepper hair on his dome.

Corbett entered followed by the Israeli Prime Minister Jairus Abramson and two secret service agents.

The president stood, came around the desk and extended his hand, which Abramson took immediately. "Prime Minister, very good to see you again. I trust your trip was pleasant."

Abramson shook Harwood's hand warmly and clamped a second over it—a sign of friendship—as he replied with a thick accent. "Very much, Mister President, and it is indeed my pleasure to see you again, as well."

Harwood gestured to nearby seats and dismissed the secret service agents along with Corbett by way of thanks.

When they were comfortable Harwood began, "I wanted to thank you again for all of the cooperation we're receiving from your people in the Mossad. The intelligence briefs I've received from the CIA Director have been most eye-opening."

Abramson nodded with a disarming grin. "Whit Jones. Good man. Were he Israeli, he'd be on my team."

"I will certainly pass that on, thank you."

"We've been concerned for some time now about the increased activities along our borders," Abramson noted.

Harwood expressed puzzlement. "I thought Mister Jones had reported you had things well in hand on that count."

"We have," Abramson nodded. "But in recent weeks, our operations have faltered. The intelligence ranks within groups along the border are growing stronger by the day. With the support of Hamas, they've begun a disinformation campaign and I am discouraged to report it has become quite effective."

"That's interesting. Any idea where they're getting their information?"

Abramson raised his hands in a stereotypical Semitic gesture. "I think it has fallen naturally out of Hamas and their political rhetoric. They are still talking about our alleged assassination attempt on Abu Na'im, an attack that occurred more than two years ago."

"And one which I know you had no part," Harwood interjected.

"That is correct. In fact, many of the members of the very ISIS-inspired terror groups they claim to be our doing are actually former disgruntled members of Hamas themselves. Many of these see Hamas as weak, and we think they may be behind the recent push to develop more sophisticated intelligence."

"They would certainly have the money and technology to back them, if what you're saying is accurate."

This was somewhat unthinkable.

It was tough enough to combat terrorism of the kind happening in places like the Gaza Strip right now. The idea that terrorists were now developing intelligence assets with some capabilities close to or even on the level of Israel and her allies terrified Harwood. It would make things more difficult for Mossad, to be sure, and the Israeli intelligence group was a major pipeline of information for the CIA and FBI.

Similar disinformation campaigns and terrorist intelligence assets could begin to build here in the United States, and the threat would become much more real if it manifested on home turf.

"I'm very glad I invited you here, Prime Minister. I have someone who could potentially help us with the growing problem if you would be willing to accept it."

"At this point, Mister President, I would be willing to accept any help you care to offer. We cannot allow this to grow beyond what it already has. I must devise a plan before less conservative elements within my government decide to exercise a stronger and more permanent option."

Harwood shuddered at the thought. The Israelis had long supported the idea of nuclear proliferation, but the use of tactical nukes wasn't beyond them.

"Then I think it's doubly important we find an alternative," Harwood replied. "And fast."

CHAPTER 3

Baltimore, Maryland

"I've acquired a contract to sell a new weapon unparalleled in human history. These new weapons have momentous, destructive potential. And I'm going to place them into the hands of the highest bidders. But first, I must eliminate my adversary."

"You do realize what you're asking. Simply hiring someone to kill the PM of Israel isn't the end of the task. It's really only the beginning."

Thaddeus Resnikoff rose from his desk. He shoved his hands in his pockets and began to walk the borders of his massive office.

"And *you* think I need to be reminded of that."

Nick Blair scowled. "No. I'm just saying this isn't the same thing as asking us to eliminate some low-ranking government hack or corporate executive."

Resnikoff may not have liked the way Blair spoke to him but the guy knew how to get the job done. And he didn't have anyone else of Blair's reputation he'd trust to pull this off.

"Not to mention the PM is probably one of the most highly protected people in the world next to the President of the United States. How the fuck do you expect me to get a whole hit team into Israel and get close enough to kill him?"

"You won't have to go to Israel!" Resnikoff said, stopping to raise a finger. "I happen to know for a fact that the prime minister is right here in the United States."

Blair cocked his head and scratched at the five o'clock shadow for which he was notoriously known to sport solely for pleasing ladies who preferred bad boys. The myriad of biker tattoos had gone unexplained since it was a fact Blair had never been a member of any known biker gang.

Not that it mattered to Resnikoff. A lot of that was just on Blair's part to build up his image. A façade, nothing more.

Resnikoff said, "But your task will still not be easy. The PM is staying at Camp David."

"What?" Blair scoffed. "We'd have a better chance if he was in Israel. Camp David is a military installation. Tons of security, virtually impenetrable, and no exterior photographs have been allowed in fifty years. Hell, even the exact location of where the president stays is unknown."

"Correction," Resnikoff said. "It *was* unknown. You see, my recent allies who are wanting to acquire these weapons were able to provide us with this information."

"In exchange for?"

Resnikoff was stone-faced. "That's none of your concern, Blair. Suffice it to say I came by the information and this will result in a...moderate discount if it pans out."

"Well you'll eat that on your own, because I won't be giving any discounts. I'm not even sure yet I want to accept."

"The deal for the information and what comes in return is between me and my client. Confidentiality rules and all that. You understand professional courtesy. Your fee will be the usual."

"My fee will be double if I take this, Resnikoff," Blair said. "And that's non-negotiable."

That's about what he figured Blair would say, and he'd already planned it in the budget. It wouldn't be a problem. Blair would be taking all the risks here. The man was a highly effective mercenary, but he was an asshole, and Resnikoff figured this would stroke Blair's ego and sense of self-importance. It wasn't anything to him, really. Resnikoff would still turn a huge profit even if he had to pay Blair triple his normal sum.

Why emasculate the guy, despite how easy it was?

Resnikoff did his best to look pained for a minute before he said, "Very well, Mister Blair. I will pay your ask. But not a penny more, regardless of any losses you might suffer. And if you don't get the job done, I expect a refund. Will the usual deposit plus say...twenty percent be sufficient?"

Blair looked mollified as he replied with a curt nod.

"You'll have the money tomorrow in your Cayman account."

"Fine." Blair sat and lit a smoke, and Resnikoff joined him. "Now how about you tell me how we're supposed to pull this off?"

"I'm merely the one providing the data," Resnikoff replied. "You're the tactician. How you choose to get it done is not my problem."

"There'll be electronic security everywhere. Not to mention heavily armed military personnel. They might even have light armor or tanks."

Resnikoff nodded with a smile. "Quite likely."

"You're really enjoying this, aren't you?" Blair asked through a gust of smoke.

"As I said, it's not my problem."

"Don't feel like you need to hide your true feelings. I know you don't like me, but I know you *need* me for this. You need the best and I'm the best."

"Let's not quibble around semantics, Blair. You're the best I could *find* on short notice."

Blair stood and smiled. "Well, I'm glad we can agree on that. You see, that's what I like most about you. You're direct. I think in other circumstances we could have been friends. Now let's get through this so I can get back to my hotel and the very young, exotic thing waiting for me there."

"I assume you've assembled your team per my specifications?"

Blair nodded. "They're ready. I think we can do this provided your information is good."

"It's good." Resnikoff sat at his desk. "I don't wish to keep you. I'll send the data via the usual secure channels. Good day."

Blair shrugged. "Suits me."

Nick Blair nearly killed himself as he skidded and slipped his way to his car, navigating the slush outside Resnikoff's headquarters, an abandoned factory on the outskirts of Baltimore. Christ but he hated the East Coast this time of year!

A storm had passed through the day before, the noonday sun melting a mess into a bigger mess. Fortunately, he'd dressed for the weather—this was a pitiful environment compared to that of his home in Palm Springs—while he considered the most recent meteorological reports.

Another storm was gauged to pass through in the next twenty-four hours, and this concerned Blair as he drove to his hotel. Then there was this whole deal with Resnikoff. When the Russian arms dealer had told him to prepare his team, he hadn't said anything about Camp David or even the target initially. Now here he had less than twelve hours to plan this and he still didn't know anything about the target.

And where the hell had Resnikoff gotten this info anyway? He wasn't going to reveal the source, but Blair wouldn't have expected that anyway. He would have to trust the information and that didn't exactly give him a warm fuzzy.

He wasn't going to worry about it now. He thought of the girl named Rica awaiting him at his hotel, her brown body sprawled across the bed. She was an escort, but he didn't care because she was *very* good and knew how to please him.

She fucked him and he paid her money—a perfect business arrangement for a mercenary.

After he arrived at the hotel and had his fill of Rica, he kicked her out and then sat at his secure computer. The information was there. All of it, just like Resnikoff had promised. There were aerial photographs showing exactly where the lodge was positioned. There were schematics of where every electronic sensor was placed. There were security rosters with names and times and dates.

That was the one thing a lot of people didn't get. The more security to manage the more information you needed to have and store. One way or another, if that information got leaked, it turned out to be an exploit in itself. The more data to track the more complex it became to manage. The larger the security footprint, the harder it was to change and adapt quickly.

Sure, they could change the rotation times and access codes and anything else they wanted, but most of that took planning. According to Resnikoff, this information was fresh and nothing major was likely to change prior to kickoff time. There were always those things one couldn't know, like fail safes and non-predictors, but Blair had conducted complex operations like this before.

Besides, they knew their target. It was simply a matter of getting in undetected. Then do the hit and get out of Dodge however and as fast as they could. Sure, the state had eyes on all of them but by the time they figured out what happened it would be too late. Blair and his men—at least those who survived—would be in the wind.

Blair continued his study of the grounds and positions of the guards and sensors. Roving patrols of three, with crossover every two hundred feet around the clock. There were both cameras and infrared. A fifteen-foot chain link fence topped with razor-wire encircled the entire property. Wind and privacy screens were woven through the fencing. There were also noise and vibration detectors.

Lesser men would have considered the place all but impenetrable, but Blair wasn't a lesser man. He was *all* man. At least that's what Rica told him, but he already knew that. Blair didn't consider guys like Resnikoff even comparable to him as a man. He didn't like that Russian turd, but the guy paid too damn well to turn away his business. Men like Resnikoff were soft—puppets of a system that had made them and bootlickers to others just like them. The guy had probably never fired a shot in his life from the weapons he dealt.

Blair looked through the aerial photographs many times, sifted the geography in his mind. Camp David was a perfect site and had been selected with obvious care by its imaginers. The ground was cold and hard and oftentimes unnavigable by any team that didn't have adequate mountaineering equipment at its disposal.

Blair had all of that and more. A couple dozen men, all veterans of multiple wars. Resnikoff, as always, had agreed to supply the weapons and munitions free of charge. That made it much easier than having to go look for that stuff. But the rest of it was another matter. Not that they couldn't get all they needed at a local outdoor shop. Resnikoff had suggested climbing equipment, rugged packs, heavy boots and thermal clothing. They would hit the place with the most advanced small arms. The cache included SMGs, pistols, grenades and nearly three hundred pounds of plastique.

It took a while, but Blair eventually spied what he sought most.

If they wanted to pull this off, they'd have to cut the power once they breached the perimeter. To less experienced eyes the entrance to the underground generator station might have been missed. Blair spotted it because he knew to look for it. Another difference between him and others Resnikoff could have hired. What a jackass, Resnikoff actually having the balls to say Blair's team was the best he could find on short notice. Like what? As if Blair didn't know what the fuck he was doing?

It didn't matter. Blair wouldn't concern himself with that fact because he had a job to do. That's how a consummate professional handled things and it was a motto by which he'd stood most of his career as first a combatant in U.S. Special Forces and later as a mercenary with a PMC. Eventually, he'd struck out on his own.

"Wait," he muttered. "What the hell is this?"

It was a note tacked on to the end by Resnikoff that read: "Reports suggest members of FF may be present. Any additional high-value targets you can score are acceptable, and subject to additional bonuses."

It took Blair a bit of time to figure out the initials as he thought through it, but he eventually mouthed the words:

First Family. Woman and children? No. That wouldn't be part of the deal. He'd terminate any opposition that posed a threat, even kill Harwood if it came to it. But he wasn't a baby or woman killer unless they had a rocket launcher pointed at him. Resnikoff was crazy if he thought Blair or any of his men would do something like that, bonuses or no bonuses. Just another example of what a coward he was.

Blair decided in that moment. Once the job was done, he would end his affiliation with Resnikoff. The guy had just crossed a line—no conscience and a complete lack of vision.

It will be all right, Blair told himself. *I've got conscience enough for both of us.*

CHAPTER 4

A brisk chill had already begun to settle on Camp David as the winter sun crawled toward dusk.

Cody and Sara began to debark from Marine Two before the rotors had wound to a stop. Cody felt the weariness settling into his bones. He'd hit the shower first, and then maybe take Sara's suggestion about a long hike. Stretching his legs and cool air would probably do him some good.

As he stood near the chopper and stretched a bit, Cody took in his surroundings. The peaked roofs of the main lodge stood off in the distance a bit. A paved walkway led from the helipad to the house, clear of ice or snow, the blue tint of the deicing agents shimmering in the afternoon light.

"First visit to Camp David?" Sara asked.

"Yes." He locked eyes with hers. They were beautiful, he had to admit, much like Carol's. It made him think of his wife in that moment, a flashback of the last time he'd seen Carol's eyes, and he averted his gaze. "You?"

"I was here once before along with Whit Jones," she replied, and she frowned as she pulled the collar of her stylish overcoat closer against her neck. "That was in the summer, though, and it was a wee bit warmer then."

"Why did we leave Shayna behind?" Cody asked.

"She wanted to ride with her family. They're all coming in by vehicles."

Cody nodded and absently replied, "Ah."

Owen McConnell exited the helicopter and immediately went into a stretching routine to mirror Cody's. "Man, but I ache."

"Getting old, Blades?" Sara asked with a snicker.

McConnell winked. "I still got some surprises left in me, young lady."

Cody agreed. McConnell was fit as a fiddle, a high requirement given his position. Blades had opted to change into his Service "A" uniform before they departed Andrews and he wore it well. Full birds gleamed against his collars. A wall of ribbon medals adorned the left breast, including the Silver Star. Crisp trousers and patent leather shoes completed the ensemble.

"Here," Sara said, turning to him. "Allow me to adjust your tie, Colonel."

"Happily."

Cody winced at the gesture, but he pushed down any retort. Sara was just being Sara and Cody wasn't about to let the feelings he'd been having about her show. Despite the time that had passed since the death of Carol and his children, he had guilt. It haunted him daily, in fact, and he was ashamed to admit these new leanings toward Sara.

He was reaching out desperately in grief, and he didn't want to make any possible relationship with Sara about that. It wasn't fair to her. She needed someone stable and steady and he wouldn't foist his broken heart upon her. Better to remain silent and let her think he was a fool than open his mouth and confirm it.

They had spoken of this before, flirting with the idea of possibly taking what they had to the next level, but Cody couldn't let that affect his judgment. He needed all his wits on every mission for which Harwood called upon him. The distractions of romance or marriage had to remain in some other place and possibly even for someone else. Besides, he didn't deserve her, and he didn't have any right to lay a burden on her. Since Carol and the kids were gone, he'd vowed to remain a loner and solo show until he found what he sought most.

Death.

Cody cracked a grin. "Even a straight tie and spiffy uniform can't do anything for a face like yours."

"Bite me, Jack," Blades said with a return smile. "And you'd be an expert on that, anyway, being a former squid and all."

"Nice comeback."

Sara rolled her eyes. "You know what I see? Two little boys trying to be the top bully in the schoolyard."

The trio laughed and then proceeded together along the walkway toward the lodge. Even this short walk by measure felt good to Cody. It helped him to feel free and lifted some of the earlier burden he'd experienced. There wasn't really any way for him to release his stress between missions other than physical activity. He didn't have much of a life and was too busy for any hobbies to speak of. Then there was his whole relationship with Sara.

And why the hell are you back to that? he thought.

They were greeted by a veritable army of secret service agents when they reached the lodge. It didn't take long to verify their credentials and they were ushered into a lounge area off the main hall. There was fresh fruit and some finger sandwiches on a table covered with white linen in one corner, along with a bowl of ice and assorted beverages.

Cody and Blades immediately helped themselves and Sara commented how they were so typically male. As soon as there was food to be had they were all over it. The pair ignored her and that only stood to verify her observations.

Both men stayed fit and as a result they had enormous appetites, respectively. Cody was on his second bottle of water and fifth tuna fish when Jim Corbett arrived. They shook hands in turn and then Corbett waved them back to their seats. He took an elegant overstuffed chair in one corner of the arranged circle, unbuttoned his coat and crossed his legs.

"How was the trip?" he asked.

"Just fine, thanks for asking, Jim."

"We had to send you Marine Two because apparently they had some sort of issue with the main bird, Owen."

Blades nodded and around a mouthful of deviled ham said,

"Yeah, I got a heads up from the crew chief. Apparently, there was a hydraulic leak, so they didn't want to clear it for flight until they repaired and conducted a full inspection."

"Wouldn't do to fly our most precious cargo on a defunct chopper," Corbett said.

Blades' mouth was full so he only chose to nod at that.

Corbett turned to Cody. "And what about you, Jack? Everything going okay?"

"Couldn't be better."

"I assume Sara filled you in on why POTUS called you here."

"She did."

"I know you're not much for ceremony."

Cody swallowed hard at the last bite and sat back in the sofa. "It's no secret but when he calls, I'm only too happy to come running."

Corbett snickered. "Yeah, well I know that's a bunch of bullshit but I'm content to let it slide."

"Jim," Sara interjected, "were you given any sort of schedule around this?"

"I don't have the details, but the rest of the first family should be here soon. There's a formal dinner scheduled for seven, and then the ceremony will be held immediately after that."

"And then?" Cody asked.

Corbett shrugged and said matter-of-factly, "Then that's it."

"So, what does he want to give me?"

"Pardon?"

"Martin. What does he want to give me?"

"I'm not sure what you mean."

"I already have a Navy Cross and more ribbons than I care to count. I don't need another one and I certainly don't need some certificate."

"I don't think that's the plan, Jack," Sara said quickly.

Corbett sat forward and put his elbows on his knees. He looked levelly at Cody and said, "Listen up, Jack. The President of the United States has asked you here as an honored guest. The least you could do is not act like a jackass about this."

"I don't know what else to be," Cody said.

"As far as I know, the president has no intention of pinning a military medal on you. This is a *personal* commendation. Now what that entails or what it means, I don't really give a shit. But what I do know is that Martin is a good man; he just wants to show you a little gratitude. So, do us all a favor and just be gracious tonight."

As Cody stood, he said, "I'm sorry if I'm not meeting with your approval on this, Corbett, but I don't answer to you. Couldn't care less if you're the chief of staff or Pocahontas. I don't want medals or favors or personal gratitude. I'm a professional operator and all I want is a little breathing room, not to be sent on stupid assignments to pull presidential daughters out of scrapes the secret service never should have let them get into to begin with."

Cody turned to look at Sara. "Look I'm sorry about this, Sara, and I'll make the appearance because I keep my word.

But for right now I think I need some air." To Blades he added, "Thanks for the lift, ace."

***

"What the hell has gotten into him?" Corbett asked.

"He's not wrong, Jim," Blades said. "He doesn't work for you."

Corbett frowned. "Now you're taking his side?"

"Maybe."

Sara sighed. "Nobody is taking anybody's side because we're all on the same side. But you need to cut him slack. Cody's just not like other people."

"Well the guy ain't bulletproof," Corbett muttered.

"Jim, please don't ever say that again," Sara countered. "Jack has been through so much and he's never done anything but give and give to a sometimes-ungrateful country."

"He's chosen to live that life," Corbett countered. "Nobody chose it for him."

"But he *does* what he does because he's in pain."

"Far be it from me to get involved in all of this but should we really be discussing this behind the guy's back?" Blades asked. "I mean, I consider him a fellow veteran and consummate pro, to make no mention that we've known each other for a long time. He's also my friend in other circumstances. I think we at least owe him the courtesy of not talking about him like a specimen under a microscope."

"I think maybe we all need to just drop the subject," Sara said.

"Yeah," Corbett replied. "I couldn't agree more."

"So, who's this mysterious guest of honor that's showed up?" Blades asked.

"It's need-to-know, and even if I could tell you it wouldn't be my news to tell."

Sara said, "Israeli Prime Minister Abramson."

Corbett did nothing to hide his surprise. "How the heck did you know that?"

"Because POTUS told me he'd be coming here," Sara said.

"Wait a minute," Blades said. "Does any of this have to do with why we were invited here?"

Corbett shook his head. "It's two separate deals. The only reason you and Sara were called here was because, as you've so eloquently pointed out, you're two of the only people who know Cody well enough that he considers you his friends. The president wanted him to have some familiar faces around because he knew this would be a bit uncomfortable."

"Not to mention the guy doesn't get out enough," said Martin Harwood.

All three rose as he entered, and Harwood waved nonchalantly at them. "Please, you all need to relax. We can skip the formalities here. Camp David is supposed to be a place of rest and relaxation where we can be on more level terms. You have entirely too many sticks up your butts."

Harwood gave Sara a peck and said, "Except you, my dear."

"Thank you, Mister President," she said sweetly. "It's good to see you."

Harwood nodded, clapped his hands and said, "Speaking

of which, where is Jack?"

A long silence followed, and Harwood finally said, "He did come. Didn't he?"

"Of course, sir," Sara replied quickly. "He was just anxious to get a shower before meeting you."

The president gave her a wry grin and said, "Um-hmm. Never lie to POTUS, Sara. I know this scene isn't for him, but I didn't bring him here to embarrass him."

"He knows that, Mister President. He just…needed a shower and a little bit of a breather. I suggested he go for a nice long walk before dinner. I'm sure his mood will lighten once he sees you and the rest of the first family."

"Very well. I guess I did kind of spring it on him. But thanks for making him tag along all the same, Sara."

"Mister President, I would like to hear how your meeting with the PM went."

"We can get into that later. I prefer not to talk shop right now. We all need to take a break from the daily grind."

"Begging your pardon, sir, but the terrorists don't take a break."

"I know," Harwood replied with an easy chuckle. "But you're just going to have to trust me for now. PM Abramson and I have significantly more to talk about before I'm ready to make any decisions. But I promise you that if it leads any-where and we need to activate Cody, that you will be my first call."

"Yes, sir."

Harwood made a point to shake McConnell's hand as well,

but not before the marine pilot came to immediate attention and saluted. They noticed that this time Harwood didn't chide Blades on formality. To do so would have been insulting to a marine, and especially Blades who was a marine's marine.

"It's good to see you, Owen."

"Mister President."

"Well, since I've already seen Jim, obviously I suppose I'd better get ready to receive the first family. Thanks again for coming and you all just relax until dinner. If you wish to clean up or anything, we'll have staff show you to your rooms. Sara, I know you didn't have time to pack but I do believe we have a number of dresses on hand for just such contingencies. I'm sure you can find one to fit you. Patrice can show you where to look."

"Thank you again, Mister President. I would very much enjoy that."

"You're quite welcome and we'll see you this evening."

CHAPTER 5

Martin Harwood stood proud as a peacock outside the lodge as the motorcade arrived.

Agents everywhere crisscrossed the grounds in very precise, redirected fashion and beyond them in the trees were armed men unmatched in their abilities as military security for Camp David.

As the first vehicle rolled to a stop and a small but athletically built female agent opened the rear door of the armored limo, the face of beautiful woman beamed at Harwood.

Pavlina Christopolous Harwood—first lady and devoted wife—dipped first one slim leg to the pavement and then the other. Black and silver were the colors of her long, elegant coiffed hair. At age fifty-eight she still had the poise and grace of a twenty-year-old. Deep, brown eyes luminesced in the twilight as she crossed the few steps to where her husband waited and delivered a proper but observed kiss full on the lips.

"Lina," Harwood greeted her, hugging her. "I'm so glad you're here."

"Of course, Love," she replied.

Despite being slight, she was full-figured in her pantsuit and wool coat, evidence she spent a lot of time golfing and walking. The thick eyebrows and large eyes belied her Greek heritage and she wore her smoky Mediterranean good looks well. Harwood was the luckiest man alive, not only because of Lina's outward and inward beauty but because she was possessed of a keen intelligence.

Behind her emerged Shayna who looked haggard, at best. She greeted her father with a kiss on the cheek and he merely smiled briefly and held a hand to the side of her flushed face. All would be discussed and forgiven in time, but Harwood would not start a scene here or scold her publicly.

She nodded in understanding of this already as he'd spoken briefly to her about it over the phone, and he was confident she'd spilled the story to her mother already. Lina would fill in any details when the three of them sat to discuss it.

Out of the second vehicle came Gary Martin Harwood, aged thirty-three and ruggedly handsome like his father. He was an industrial engineer for a large firm in the heart of Washington, D.C. First-born to Martin and Lina, his wife Greta accompanied him with their three-year-old daughter, Tina, in tow. The little girl was undoubtedly the pride and joy of her grandfather and no less spoiled. She ran to Harwood who smiled at her and picked her up in his arms before shaking the hand of his son and placing a peck on Greta's cheek.

"Come inside all of you and let's get you warmed up," he said.

The first family followed him into the lodge, and they were greeted by an entourage of staff who took coats, hats, and boots in various flavors from the brood.

Harwood continued holding little Tina as they filed into the sitting room.

"Marianna is right behind us, dear," Lina told Harwood. "Her flight was delayed."

Harwood smiled when he thought of his fiercely independent middle daughter. She'd had the hardest time of it amongst the other members of the first family. Her anti-political stance had been there long before Harwood became president. She could have been further along in her figure-skating career at twenty-nine, but the loner streak in her sometimes held her back. Marianna's lack of advancement had been a constant source of angst for her.

"There's sandwiches and snacks if any of you are hungry," Harwood said. "We'll not eat for a couple of hours yet."

"Hey, Dad, let me take her off your hands," Greta said. "I'd like to see if she'll take a nap before dinner."

Harwood gave up Tina immediately but with visible reluctance. Greta swiped with a bare hand at the bit of drool that had run from Tina's mouth, through her fingers and dropped on the breast of Harwood's suit coat.

Harwood didn't appear to mind but all the first family realized that while he might be Dad, he was also the most powerful man in the free world, and it wouldn't do for him to look anything less than his absolute best.

"Martin, you should get out of that suit anyway," Lina suggested firmly but lovingly. "This is Camp David, not the Oval Office. Learn to relax a little."

Harwood laughed as he touched his wife's hand. "And here I was just giving that same advice to Owen and Sara not ten minutes ago."

"Sara's here?"

Harwood nodded.

"Oh, I so love her. She's such a gentle and sweet soul."

"Agreed."

Lina lowered her voice some and asked, "Is he here? Did he come?"

"Yes."

"That's good...very good," Lina said with a small sigh. "That man needs to surround himself with better things and times."

Lina knew all about Jack Cody, at least what it was safe for her to know. Her husband withheld nothing from her as she was his most trusted friend and ally. She didn't know details of anything around his personal life other than he'd lost his family to a "tragic accident" and that's all Harwood would tell her. But she somehow knew, that keen intuition of hers being what it was, so it worked out because Harwood could give a small detail and Lina could easily glean the rest.

Of course, Shayna had also surely revealed everything that occurred in Fort Lauderdale. Lina knew, as did the entire family, that Cody was no choir boy. One look at him could imply this to even a halfwit. Cody carried an aura of power and command with him, as well as a few visible scars.

"How's work, Son?" Harwood asked Gary.

The thirty-three year old, who had retrieved a Coke for himself and chilled glass of Rosette for his wife, nodded. "Good, really good. I might be looking at a promotion to VP soon."

"That's excellent news!" Harwood boomed. He shook his son's hand warmly and said, "Congratulations. I had no doubts you'd be a success in whatever you did."

Gary smiled and stood a little taller and straighter. "Thanks."

He'd always been a gentle boy, but Gary had a superior intellect. He'd known from a very early age he wanted to be in some type of engineering. Martin and Lina both surmised he'd end up in aerospace, so it came as a surprise when he chose industrial engineering as his desired trade. Despite it all, Gary was no less successful. He made very good money as a man with his talents and intelligence was wont to do, and he treated his family well. Greta adored him and was never shy about saying or showing it.

Harwood let his eyes rove around the room and felt his chest might burst through his coat. This was the first family, *his* family, and he could not have been more proud of each of them. They were for the most part well-adjusted and success-ful with maybe the exception of Shayna's foibles.

Shayna Harwood was just another story entirely and her father couldn't understand it. She had so much to offer the world, being bright like her mother and educated. She'd achieved high honors in college, but she'd returned from school somewhat restless and under-eager. Harwood hadn't been able to put his finger on it, but maybe after they talked it would become clear enough that Martin and Lina could figure out how to help Shayna get on a good path.

Or at least a better one.

Jack Cody decided he'd take a shower on his return. What he needed most right now was to get some isolation and think things through.

As he walked, he resigned himself to find a good opportunity to apologize to Jim Corbett. He'd not really had any cause to speak to POTUS's chief of staff that way, irrespective of the reasons. It wouldn't serve any purpose not to get along with the staff, and especially not on this occasion.

Cody knew Harwood understood—really, they all understood—the torment he'd been through even if they'd not experienced such tragedy themselves.

But "Suicide" Cody wasn't a man who needed pity or friendship that could salve the consciences of others. What he *really* needed was a mission so he could get back into his element and maybe get himself one step closer to that final exit for which he so longed. Here he was, closest to some of the most powerful and influential people on the planet, and he didn't give a shit.

Since Cody had never been to Camp David before, he

decided to confine his walk to the long drive that led from one of the entry points straight to the lodge. Besides, trudging through the snow wouldn't have been wise. It could set off the vibration sensors, and even though he knew the secret service had told the guard contingent that Cody would be walking, it wouldn't do to go trudging through the snow, setting off alarms, and taking any attention from a real threat.

Cody was an avid hiker, but he wasn't a stupid asshole.

Along the trail he spotted several of the sentries. It's not like they were hiding but Cody thought it a bit sloppy, nonetheless. He just approached those kinds of tactical details differently. They had been doing this long enough that he didn't need to worry about it. Better to just walk, breathe, and mind his own goddamn business.

Far ahead he saw a vehicle approaching, the light having waned enough to turn the sky gray, so it had its headlights on. He stepped off the roadway and into the snow, intent to remain motionless until the vehicle passed. Instead it slowed to a stop and the rear window rolled down. A face adorned by brown hair and spotted with freckles stared back at him. The young woman had the familiar good looks of her mother, but the intent gaze was her dad's.

"Jack Cody," Marianna said in an almost matter-of-fact way.

Cody lent her a half-grin as he stepped onto the road and up to the vehicle. He put one hand on the armored roof and bent slightly so he could get eye-level. In a like tone to hers he replied, "Marianna Harwood."

Cody liked Marianna a lot and she felt equally friendly toward him. They'd treated their relationship as somewhat of a secret, although they didn't do anything to outwardly hide it as much as just didn't speak about it. Outside of Sara, Blades, and POTUS, Cody had a unique relationship with the Harwood's middle daughter.

She was smart and sassy but could be very gentle and kind when she put her mind to it. Cody had hoped, like the rest of the first family, that she would eventually hit a career success but so far it hadn't materialized. Marianna hadn't spoken much of this to her family, but she'd confided it to Cody.

He appreciated her candor and good sense. She was never shy about her political views, which were basically she didn't have any, and that was another facet of her unique personality Cody liked. She had no time for bullshit, giving or receiving, and always seemed to be able to easily meet people wherever they were at without judgment.

Jack Cody counted Marianna as one of his few friends.

"So, what did Daddy promise in order to drag you out to this shindig?" she asked with a broad smiled that highlighted the laugh lines around her eyes. It made her grin infectious.

Cody scratched at the back of his neck as he replied, "Not really my news to tell. I guess he wants to thank me, but nobody seems to know how he plans to do it."

"For?"

"I think you should ask him, Squirt."

She nodded and sighed. "Well, I'm sure whatever it's for, you've got it coming."

"I hate ceremony," he replied with a furrowed brow.

"I know, that's I mean." She chuckled. "You've got it coming."

"You're a brat."

"You're a doll."

Cody said, "How come you didn't come with the rest of the family?"

"My flight in from Heathrow was delayed." Marianna had been living in the United Kingdom for the last few months, training. "I'm trying to get ready for this minor league summit. I'm hoping this will be the one that puts me on the map."

"You know, I'm sure it's no secret to you in what capacity I serve your dad."

She shrugged. "I could guess if it really mattered to me that much. I don't care what you do for a living. You know I like you, Jack."

"I do. And you know I care about you and want the best for you. But if I've learned anything after all this time from life, from all the things I've seen and done, it's that you should *never* hold yourself back. Never doubt. Things will work out if you just believe in yourself."

"Who are you?" she interjected. "Yoda?"

Cody laughed and he was grateful for it. "Smart ass kid. What I'm trying to tell you is that you should attempt to achieve whatever it is in life for yourself and believe you can do it. Don't do it for anyone else, Marianna. You've got a lot to offer the world by just being yourself. You do that, the rest will come."

"Yes, professor," she said and winked. "So, what are you

doing out here?"

Cody looked off to the distance. "Taking a walk. Clearing my head."

"Shouldn't take long."

"Hilarious. You should get to the lodge."

"Later, Jack."

Cody rapped his knuckles on the roof and the armored SUV pulled away immediately.

CHAPTER 6

The back of the truck smelled of extra gun oil mixed with sweating men.

The temperature had dropped rapidly but Nick Blair had already planned for this. His men were hardened professionals, every one of them handpicked for this job. All of the equipment was in place and the strategy set.

Blair banged on the back of the truck to indicate the driver should stop at this point.

They had selected a modified Volkswagen cargo truck imported from Mexico, and stripped it of any identification. Blair had arranged to scatter a few of them on hand in key locations throughout the US, bought and imported by a toymaker shell company.

Their armament was varied—including MP5 SMGs, a couple of Colt carbine assault rifles equipped with under-barrel 40 mm grenade launchers, and H&K PSG1 sniper rifles, assorted grenades of both type HE fragmentation and thermite, and heavy plastiques.

They would need to use a special case of detonating cord to breach the fence.

Timing would be everything and they would have to make their approach from the hill side of the mountains. This gave them the high ground and allowed them to approach closely enough to hopefully avoid setting off the vibration sensors. Even if they did, the Catoctin Mountain Park was known for its active wildlife. As long as they moved carefully and quietly, took their time, they should be able to close on the perimeter undetected.

Ten men exited the VW truck and formed on their point man with Blair in third position.

Blair sensed their apprehension, the tension in the air almost palpable. Most of the jobs he'd done had been conducted in other countries. Domestic operations of this size weren't something for which Blair had a lot of appetite, but Resnikoff had agreed to pay for the extra inconvenience so he could live with it this one time.

The travel over several miles of rocky, nearly knee-deep snow was slow and grueling. Every step had to be calculated and progress wouldn't be speedy. They couldn't use flashlights and the only one with a night-device was the point man, so Blair had to follow the man's every step and pass the same pathway back to the group with hand signals.

Blair glanced at his chronometer at one point: coming up on 0123 hours. If he'd calculated correctly, they could make fence side by 0330. The wind grew colder and more intense as they advanced, biting into the men mercilessly. They wore ample protective clothing with ultra-thin thermals beneath their snow-mountain camouflage fatigues and coats. They'd opted to forego helmets, but their balaclavas were reinforced with the thinnest Kevlar available.

Step after agonizing step, Blair ran every possible variable through his mind on a continuous cycle. No words had to be or were spoken. On his neoprene gloves, Blair had sewn nightglow strips into the fingers of his gloves. All of the men could read the codes from there.

Fist: stop.

Waggle fingers: slow down.

Twirled index finger: speed up.

Flat palm: hunker.

The list went on, but Blair knew to keep it simple. The simpler, the better, because they could operate smoothly and noiselessly as possible. And so, they continued on like a chain-gang of ghosts.

With death and destruction as their prizes.

Sleep eluded Cody.

He'd tossed and turned for more than three hours and finally climbed from bed, dressed in heavy khaki pants, thick wool socks, and a black sweater. Then he sat in a chair by the window. The fuzzy glow emanating from the bedside clock was his only bright companion. Pipes faintly creaked but it was quiet enough the most deafening sound in the room ended up being his own shallow breathing.

Cody stared out the window and meditated—his muscles had finally relaxed but his mind remained alert. Some sense he couldn't identify gnawed at his gut. Deep shadows seemed to play at the corners of his eyes. He wasn't feeling sleepiness. He knew this one. Loneliness and isolation. The grief had locked him up like a prisoner in his own mind.

He needed action. He needed release.

Finally, Cody stood and clipped a leather hip holster to the right side of his belt. He went to his pillow and retrieved his Beretta M9A3, tucked it into his holster and then donned his wool coat and a stevedore's stocking cap.

For a big man he could move as silently as a snake through tall grass. He walked down the long hallway of the bedroom suites, hearing a snore there or the faint rustle of a body turning in bed, and eventually emerged in the main foyer.

A secret service agent looked up from his chair in surprise, obviously not having heard Cody's approach.

"Taking a walk," Cody said.

The agent nodded as Cody proceeded through the front door unmolested and out into the icy night. He decided to take the same path down the road initially that he had the previous evening. Every once in a while, the hardened snow and ice would crunch loudly beneath his boots. In his peripheral vision he spotted the occasional movement of a rabbit or squirrel.

No birds sounded or moved, and Cody knew this signaled the approach of more foul weather. He didn't give a care for how far he went or even whether he could find his way back. His trek became thoughtless, mechanical. The cold burned his face and Cody zipped up the coat completely, so he didn't risk frostbite.

He had to pull occasionally at the frost forming on his lower lashes from the heat escaping his breath behind the collar. No sweat, a minor irritation and walked on.

Cody couldn't be sure how far he'd gone or how much time had passed, but he knew he'd progressed much farther than planned. The wind had died some and an eerie type of stillness had come over his surroundings. Almost deathly quiet.

Calm before the storm, he thought.

Then he saw it. It was just a glimmer at first, an all too familiar wisp of movement. But it was there, and he knew it well. His gut churned and neck hairs stood up. This was no chill from the cold night air. This was danger.

CHAPTER 7

Nick Blair trusted his mercenaries—to a point. All men who fight for money have been vaguely suspect throughout human history, from pre-Christian Carthage to modern private military contractors, but that was only natural.

Why wouldn't men who fought for cash switch sides and join the highest bidder when the chips were down?

The trick to beating that, Blair knew, was paying more than anybody else and hiring only those who ranked a cut above the stragglers and deserters who had always drifted in war's wake.

The force he led tonight was small in numbers, but each member of the strike team was a kind of army in himself, ex-members of the world's top military units, hardened in the forge of down-and-dirty warfare.

Tony Graham and Ben Laughlin were the Brits, both packing the Heckler & Koch MP5 submachine guns and Glock 17MB pistols they'd wielded as members of the United Kingdom's elite striking forces. Graham had been SAS—the British Army's Special Air Service, organized in 1941, fighting their way from Hitler's Fortress Europe to the Falkland Islands, the Persian Gulf and Iraq. Laughlin had come up through Royal Navy ranks to serve the SBS—Special Boat Service—another venerable unit that had seen action this century from Sierra Leone to Afghanistan, Libya and Nigeria.

Adriaan Coetzee, armed tonight with a Colt Mark 18 CQBR/M203 and a Vektor SP1 pistol, had done time with his homeland's "Recces", the South African Special Forces Brigade, formed as the counterinsurgency "Hunter Group" in 1968, reborn after Apartheid's fall to safeguard the country's borders and political leaders, helping crush the Congo's M23 rebellion in 2012 and '13, with sidelines in stalking and liquidating high-value targets wherever they might go to ground.

Blair's German, Hans Behrens, had proved himself with the Kommando Spezialkräfte—Special Forces Command, or KSK for short—on joint anti-terror operations ranging from the fractured Balkans to Middle East. Tonight, he carried an H&K MP5 SMG, backed up with the same manufacturer's USP Tactical sidearm, plus the same grenades each of his comrades wore clipped to belts and combat webbing.

The team's Frenchman, Marcel Bouchez, was a decorated alumnus of his country's Commandement des forces spéciales Terre, translated to English as the Army Special Forces Command. For this outing, he'd chosen a Colt Mark 18/M203 heavy hitter, with a Heckler & Koch USP9 pistol snugged into the holster on his tactical vest.

Blair's play-for-pay *paisan* was Nino Nazzari, who'd made his bones and then some with Italy's Comando Subacquei ed Incursori—abbreviated COMSUBIN, translating into the Raiders and Divers Group. Tonight, with the majority of Blair's commandos, he'd selected the popular Colt Mark 18/M203 but deviated for his backup weapon, picking a Glock 19 pistol that was standard issue from his COMSUBIN days.

The team's point man was Dion O'Reilly, an Irishman from County Sligo, who'd earned his spurs with Erin's ARW, the Army Ranger Wing. A long-range marksman by training and temperament, O'Reilly carried one of their two H&K PSG1 sniper rifle, with a USP pistol riding his right hip, ready for any emergencies.

South America's contribution to the Camp David raid was Brazilian Cesar da Costa, late of the 1º Batalhão de Forças Especiais, known beyond his homeland's borders as the 1st Special Forces Battalion. Recruits who survived that unit's forty-one weeks of rigorous training emerged as experts with hardware ranging from heavy weapons and explosives to daggers and machetes. For tonight's do-or-die hoedown, da Costa packed a Mark 18 CQBR/M203 and a Taurus PT92 pistol.

Finally, a pair of hard-case Americans rounded off Blair's team. Thomas Altman had learned his killing trade with the U.S. ARMY'S 1st Special Forces Operational Detachment-Delta—"Delta Force" for short—armed tonight with another of their Colt Mark 18s and a Beretta M9 sidearm. Last but far from least came Fabius Worthy, an African American ex-U.S. Navy SEAL. Another veteran sniper, he carried the team's other H&K PSG1, with the same company's Mark 23 pistol in reserve.

Ten hard men against a small army, targeting a hard site deemed "impenetrable" by its planners over time. Nick Blair not only held the operation's purse strings but was also confident that he could hold his own against the mercs who'd signed on with him, if it came to that.

Approaching Camp David's first line of resistance, he didn't hesitate, but harked back to his childhood days in Sunday school, adding a twist to Psalms 23:4.

Yea, though I walk through the valley of the shadow of death, I will fear no evil, for I am the baddest son of a bitch in the valley.

If anyone had asked, Jack Cody couldn't have explained exactly why he brought his favorite Beretta on a nighttime stroll around Camp David. Call it force of habit, maybe even second nature, if a motive was required.

He absolutely hadn't come expecting trouble, much less an attack upon the president's retreat, crawling with military guards and secret service agents, plus agents of Mossad assigned to safeguard Tel Aviv's prime minister. How many men and guns in all? Cody had made no effort to find out.

Mossad—"The Institute", in Hebrew—was the Western world's second largest intelligence agency, its seven thousand acknowledged employees accounting for roughly one-third of the CIA's twenty-one thousand and change. Bankrolled by ten billion shekels—$2.73 billion at today's exchange rate—Mossad was responsible for intelligence gathering, disinformation, venture capital operations and executive protection, while running two separate counterterrorist units, Kidon ("Tip of the Spear") and Metasada (the Special Operations Division), both staffed by expert assassins and saboteurs. CIA headquarters credited Kidon alone with some 2,700 targeted killings since its creation in the mid-1970s, and no one at Langley believed they had seen the full picture.

The bottom line: Camp David should have ranked among the most secure facilities on Earth. And yet...

That didn't always prove to be the case, of course. During the week surrounding Independence Day in 2011, U.S. Air Force F-15 Eagle tactical fighters had intercepted three separate civilian aircraft encroaching on restricted airspace over the presidential retreat. Each in turn was escorted to Hagerstown Regional Airport, where the pilots and their passengers were grilled until authorities determined that they post no threat to anyone except, perhaps, themselves.

Hikers also turned up from time to time, roaming aimlessly through Catoctin Mountain Park's 6,164 wilderness acres. None had yet been prosecuted, pleading ignorance of Camp David's location since it appeared on no maps issued by the National Park Service, yet unsubstantiated rumors of vanishing trespassers lingered in the nearby Maryland communities of Emmitsburg and Thurmont, Maryland.

Jack Cody didn't know if those stories had any truth to them or not, but he had learned to trust the evidence of his own senses. And right now, those battle-honed instincts were working overtime.

Granted, the early morning darkness and Camp David's wooded grounds worked to obstruct him, but grim experience had taught Cody to trust his gut, along with eyes and ears that hadn't let him down so far.

If they had failed him anywhere along life's rocky road to this point, he'd be fertilizing wildflowers by now.

The problem was interpreting exactly what he'd seen and heard that set his nerves on edge.

At first, there'd been a whisper of a sound he couldn't place, then faint lights off among the trees, beyond the property's high-voltage fence crowned with a double roll of razor wire. Next came a luminescent flickering, as if someone had dipped his fingertips in black light phosphorescent paint before pretending to conduct a silent orchestra.

What in the hell?

The next intrusion on Cody's senses wiped out any latent doubt concerning peril. That time, when the light flashed with a sizzling sound, he knew it must be detonating cord.

Any modern soldier knew about det cord: a thin, flexible plastic tube filled with explosive PETN, burning at a rate of sixty-four hundred meters per second—fast enough to blow linked charges almost simultaneously even when they had been planted many yards apart. Even without those larger charges, det cord generated heat enough to melt through various defenses—say a chain-link fence, for instance—like a giant zipper being tugged open.

And if the fence in question was electrified, that flame-out broke the circuit, rendering its deadly punch harmless.

Cody needed no more proof of an invasion under way, but how should he react?

His first impulse was to engage the trespassers, but that meant facing unknown odds with only his Beretta, fifteen Parabellum rounds inside its magazine and one more in the chamber. Two spare mags under his right arm gave him forty-six shots altogether, but he likely wouldn't have a chance against the still-unseen strike team before they cut him down.

So...what?

Zapping the fence would trigger an alarm inside Camp David's secret service headquarters. Agents who hadn't seen the flare of light or heard its sizzle would be sent out to investigate at once—and they would likely walk into an ambush well before they reached the ruptured span of fencing.

Thinking fast, he drew his pistol, sighted down its slide toward darkness speckled by the det cord's after-image, and squeezed off three shots in rapid fire. He had no realistic hope of hitting anyone and didn't hang around to find out if he had.

Before the creepers could return fire, Cody was already sprinting back toward the nearest of the presidential compound's residential clusters, roughly half a mile away.

✳✳✳

Dogwood Cabin, Camp David

Sara Durell was used to seeing honchos from the Company let down their hair on holidays—the office Christmas party, or a barbecue for Independence Day at Clemyjontri Park, near Langley—but she hadn't done a lot of socializing with the Company's director and the White House chief of staff. Lounging on comfortable furniture by firelight, sipping Bushmills single malt, aged twenty-one years, impressed her as more than a tad surreal.

Whit Jones was droning on about some breakthrough in U.S.-Israeli relations, sure as he could be that just a few more billion dollars wired to Tel Aviv couldn't be viewed by any reasonable soul as pandering for votes at home, the overhead lights dimmed, cut out for just a second, then came back.

"What's that about?" James Corbett asked the room at large.

Sara knew what her companions should have realized at once. "We've had a power cut," she said. "The backup generators just kicked in."

"The storm, you think?" asked Jones.

"It wasn't snowing when we finished dinner," she reminded both men.

"Okay," Corbett said. "What is it, then?"

As if answering his question, an alarm began to sound throughout the building. It was muted, having more in common with the *ding* of an arriving elevator than the clamor of a hotel fire drill, but persistent, and accompanied by blinking amber lights in every chamber of the house.

In case her boss and Jones still didn't understand, Sara

informed them, "That means there's a breach somewhere on the perimeter."

"A breach?" Whit seemed to have forgotten basic English, or else he'd decided to play dumb. "What kind of breach?"

"It means exactly what I said," she answered back. "The Secret Service will be scrambling by now."

Most Americans were vague on what the U.S. Secret Service did and didn't do. They were aware of the security details assigned to past and current presidents, vice presidents, their spouses and immediate families. Unknown to some, the same protection extended to major presidential and vice-presidential candidates since Bobby Kennedy's assassination back in 1968, later expanded further to include foreign heads of state on American soil. Fewer still recognized the agency's involvement on occasions designated National Special Security Events by the Office of Homeland Security.

Only a handful—most of them historians—would now recall that the Secret Service began life as an arm of the Treasury Department, chasing counterfeiters during and beyond the Civil War, a duty that it still pursued today. The Service also had a uniformed division working in tandem with Washington's U.S. Capitol Police, visibly safeguarding the White House Complex; the vice president's residence at Number One Observatory Circle, on the northeast grounds of the U.S. Naval Observatory; the main Treasury Building and Annex; plus foreign embassies and diplomatic missions in the D.C. area.

The Uniformed Division stood out front, while plain-clothes agents stayed low-key, some armed with sniper rifles, automatic weapons, and shoulder-fired FIM-92 Stinger missiles, ready to take out any clear and present danger anywhere between ground level and an aircraft ceiling altitude of forty thousand feet.

Whit Jones's voice cut through her thoughts, saying, "We're safe in here, though, right?"

"You're asking the wrong lady," Sara said, already on her feet and moving toward the parlor's exit and the corridor beyond.

"Where are you going, Sara?" Corbett asked. He didn't sound exactly worried yet, although his voice had edged an octave past concerned.

"Just realized there's something I forgot, sir," she replied, already at the door, with her hand on the knob.

"What's that, pray tell?" the DCI inquired.

"My gun," she said, and left the bureaucrats behind, both gaping after her.

✳✳✳

Aspen Lodge, The Presidential Suite

President Harwood had pajamas on, was seated on the grand king bed and watching his wife brush her hair when the alarm sounded. He'd been about to compliment her on the negligee she'd chosen—one of his top favorites—when chimes and a revolving amber light smothered the mood.

Five second later, rapping on the door preceded a man's voice calling to him, "Mister President? We have a situation, sir."

Rising, Harwood grabbed Lina's silk robe from the bed beside him, where he'd hoped her negligee would soon have joined it, handed it to her and said, "I hate to say it, but I think you'd better cover up."

Outside their door, the same voice called again, louder this time. "Sir? Can you hear me? If you don't answer—"

"I'm coming, Lee," Harwood advised the chief of his protective detail, hesitating at the door just long enough to see Lina belting her robe.

Lee Wilkins was Head of Security for Martin Harwood's personal security detail. A burly African American, he stood six-five and weighed two hundred twenty pounds, resembling the football lineman that he'd been at Notre Dame while working on his prelaw studies, prior to graduating cum laude from Georgetown University Law School. Behind him stood his number two and head of Lina's Secret Service detail, Maggie Chin, who barely came to Lee's shoulder but held a black belt in mixed martial arts and was a dead-eye gunfighter who'd killed a pair of neo-Nazi counterfeiters prior to switching from investigations to executive protection.

"What's the ruckus, Lee?" Harwood demanded.

"Still uncertain, sir," Wilkins replied. "We have a fence breached at the property's southwest perimeter and a report of shots fired from the same location. We're responding, but we need to escort you and the first lady to a more secure location, sir, asap."

"Do we have time to dress?" the president inquired.

"Should be all right, sir. Quick and casual will do for now."

For the first time, Harwood glanced down and saw that Wilkins held a Remington 1100 semiautomatic twelve-gauge shotgun in his left hand, muzzle pointed to the floor.

Harwood lowered his voice, asking, "Is it that serious?"

"We hope not, sir. Still, best to be prepared."

"Five minutes, Lee," the president replied, and closed the door on his defenders.

"Martin?" Already at their shared closet, selecting warm casual clothes, Lina asked him, "How bad is it?"

"Sounds like we won't know for a while," Harwood replied. Then, since he'd never tried to shield her from the truth before, he added, "Someone's made it past the outer fence, from what I understand."

"I thought that was supposed to be impossible."

"These days," he said, "I'm not sure that word still applies to anything."

Shedding the negligee, she'd already donned lacy underthings and had the jacket of a trademark pants suit in her left hand, reaching for the slacks to match.

"We're going to the bunker, then?" While trying to stay upbeat, Lina's tone told him she hated that idea.

"For just a little while."

"It's like a tomb down there," she said.

"A pretty cushy one, all things considered."

"Even so. Is someone with the children?"

Hardly children now, the POTUS thought, but kept it to himself. Instead, he answered, "You know that they're covered all the time."

"Like Shayna was, down in Fort Lauderdale?"

"They're not a thousand miles away tonight, Lina. They're covered. Trust me."

"I do, Martin," she replied, forcing a smile devoid of mirth. "It's all the rest who worry me. What is it, seven billion now?"

"Going on eight, I think," Harwood replied.

"And how many guards do we have around the compound?"

Martin Harwood didn't know offhand and didn't feel like making up a number from thin air. "I'd have to check with Lee on that," he said.

"Exactly," Lina answered him. "And *that's* what worries me."

***

Holly Cabin

"I tell you I *must* go to see the president at once!"

There was a cutting edge of steel in to Jairus Abramson's voice, but he was getting nowhere so far with the chief of his security detail.

Naftali Sharett met his ultimate commander's level gaze without blinking.

"Mister Prime Minister," he said, "you understand that in a crisis, sir, your wishes are subordinate to matters of security."

"You speak as if this were a crisis, Captain."

"Which it *is,* sir. Interruption of electric power and phone service, the alarms, reports of gunfire from the southwest quadrant of the compound."

"All of that explains precisely *why* I must contact President Harwood."

"Not if that means placing you at greater risk, sir."

"You're refusing my direct order, Captain?"

"I am, sir. Under prevailing statutes and my standing orders from *HaKabinet HaMedini-Bithoni,* I have no legal alternative."

Aronson blinked at hearing Sharett invoke the name of Israel's State Security Cabinet. The prime minister understood his homeland's regulations, having drafted some of them himself while serving four terms in the Knesset, Israel's unicameral legislature. He understood that even a prime minister must sometimes follow orders from subordinates assigned by the Mossad to keep him safe.

"What shall we do, then, Captain?" he inquired, keeping his voice as calm as he could manage in these circumstances.

"Your team is presently on full alert, sir," Sharett said. "You should be safe here for the moment, but if any more shooting occurs, then I must relocate you to the basement shelter."

"Hiding like a frightened peasant in the Warsaw ghetto from *Obersturmbannführer* Eichmann's manhunters?"

"Eichmann was hanged in 1962, sir, and his ashes scattered in the Med. Our enemies today are more persistent and potentially more dangerous."

Abramson knew when he'd been beaten at his own game

and ceased arguing. Instead, he asked Sharett, "May I at least be trusted with a weapon to defend myself, Captain?"

"Sir, your defenders are well armed enough."

Abramson could not challenge that assertion. He, along with every other officeholder in Israel, knew that protective agents carried Jericho 941 semiauto pistols as standard equipment, most also armed with Uzi submachine guns, and a smaller number carrying Tavor X95 bullpup assault rifles. As befit a small nation surrounded by foes on every side, all of those weapons and more were manufactured by Israel Weapon Industries of Ramat HaSharon, ensuring that no foreign boycott could ever leave Israel defenseless.

Still, Abramson felt honor bound to press his point.

"Not even one small pistol, Captain?" he inquired. "You should know that I served two tours of duty with the IDF in Lebanon before first seeking public office."

The IDF, as every faithful Jew around the world knew, was the conglomerate Israeli Defense Forces, including the army, air force and navy. Abramson joined the army as an infantryman and retired with a *sgan aluf*'s rank, equivalent to a NATO lieutenant colonel, after receiving a Medal of Valor, his nation's highest military decoration.

"As you say, I am aware, sir."

"Captain, as one soldier to another, can you not trust me to hold a pistol?"

Stone-faced, Sharett turned to one of the three subordinates ranged behind him and nodded. "Do it," he commanded, a sergeant instantly stepped forward, drew a handgun from beneath his blazer—seemingly a spare, since Abramson still saw one in his shoulder holster—and presented it to the prime minister.

The IWI Jericho 941 weighs 2.9 pounds with sixteen 9×19mm Parabellum rounds in its magazine and one in the chamber. It is patterned after the well-respected Czech CZ-75, with a single- or double-action trigger, and measures eight inches long. Each of its bullets weighed eight grams and travels 1,154 feet per second, striking targets with 364 foot-pounds of energy.

Hefting the weapon in his strong right hand, Abramson told Captain Sharett, "Thank you. I feel much better now."

And wished with all his heart that it was not a lie.

Laurel Lodge

"What were you thinking, ducking your security detail that way?" asked Marianna Harwood.

Putting on the sulky face that Marianna knew so well, her younger sister Shayna answered, "Just because you're older doesn't mean that you're in charge of me. In case you missed the memo, I'm a grown-up woman, Sis."

"You're right, as far as the chronology's concerned, but will you ever start to act grown-up?"

"This, coming from the figure skater." Shayna stopped just short of sneering.

"Let me guess. You watched *The Cutting Edge* again, between your bouts of ecstasy with what's-his-name down in Fort Lauderdale?"

"His name, as you know goddamned well, is Mason."

"Right. Mason Narmy. Did you know that 'narmy' is a slang nickname for gerbils?"

"Jesus, Marianna. Get your nose out of the online Urban Dictionary, could you?"

"Shorten it to 'narm,' and do you know what that gives you?"

This time, Shayna *did* sneer. "Sorry, missed that lesson. But I'm sure you'll fill me in, right?"

"Be glad to, Sis. 'Narm' means a moment that's intended to be serious but doesn't cut it, due to sappiness, absurdity, or sloppy execution, becoming unintentionally funny."

"How much time did you waste looking that up? Maybe you should spend more time on camel spins and Salchow jumps, instead of playing babysitter."

"I'm simply saying—"

"More bullshit that I don't want to hear, okay? Instead of playing name games, maybe you should learn that Mason's a respected NSA codebreaker."

"And by taking you to Florida, he almost got you kidnapped, maybe even killed. You're only breathing now because our parents sent Cody down to find you."

"Right. Let's not forget the white knight on his charger, Marianna."

"Have you ever felt one second's gratitude for anything, Shayna?"

"You want me to be *grateful* Mom and Dad have got a mercenary stalking me?"

"He's not—"

"I saw him kill two men, all right?"

"While they were shooting up your boyfriend's hotel suite, with you and him inside it."

"Listen, I'm glad to be alive, okay?"

"You might try showing it for once, instead of getting pissed off with the ones who care about you."

"Mason cares about me, damn it! Just because you're carrying some kind of torch for Cody doesn't mean—"

Before Shayna could finish that insult, the lights flicked off, then came back seeming dimmer. At the same time, an alarm began sounding and the embattled sisters glanced up at an amber light flashing above the door to Marianna's suite.

"What's this, now?" Shayna asked.

"Trouble," her sister said. "We need to find out where our Secret Service agents are and what they know about it."

She was halfway to the door when urgent knocking sounded on the other side of it. A voice that Marianna recognized as Secret Service agent Rupert Malcolm's, called out through the panel, saying, "Mizzes Harwood, this is—"

"I know who you are, Rupert," said Marianna, as she pulled the door open.

Malcolm was thirty-odd years old, athletic in appearance, and chief of the Secret Service team assigned to guard the Harwood sisters while they stayed at Camp David. Though Marianna had been dealing with him off and on since last Inauguration Day, this was the first time she had seen him with a firearm in his hands. Tonight, he held a futuristic-looking automatic weapon, probably a submachine gun, though she couldn't name it or recite its military nomenclature.

"So, I take it this is serious," she said, frowning.

"It's not a drill, ma'am."

"Please don't 'ma'am' me, Rupert."

"Sorry, Miz Harwood. Is your sister with you?"

"Right here," Shayna answered for herself and stepped into his line of sight. "Don't tell me we were talking after curfew."

"No, ma'am."

"Hey!" Shayna protested. "I'm younger than *she* is."

"Understood, Miz Harwood." Before either of them could derail his train of thought again, Malcolm pressed on. "Something or someone, as yet unidentified, has breached the camp's perimeter about two hundred yards from here. We've had shots fired but no reports of any injuries so far."

"Shots fired," Marianna echoed. "Are you sure about that?"

"That's affirmative," Malcom replied. "We need to relocate the two of you right now."

"Hold on there," Shayna said. "You're taking us *outside*?"

"No, ma'am. You're going downstairs, to the building's basement level."

"I hate basements," Shayna warned him.

"This one's been remodeled since the old days, ma'am. It used to be a bomb shelter, but now it's more like a rec room."

"You mean a panic room," said Marianna.

"There's no reason you should panic, Miz Harwood,"

Malcolm replied. "We've got you covered, but we need to go downstairs right now."

Reluctantly, she nodded, turned and saw her younger sister's shrug of acquiescence.

At the same time as her mind was asking her, *Where's Jack? Exactly where in Hell is he?*

***

Cody, at that very moment, was three hundred yards to the southwest of Camp David's Aspen Lodge. As he jogged through frosty darkness, his Beretta holstered for the moment, Cody sorted through his knowledge of camp's facilities.

Aspen Lodge was the president's normal retreat, a split-level with six bedrooms and five baths, living and dining rooms, kitchen and pantry, with a spacious tool shed adjoining the lower terrace. Nearby stood the Evergreen Chapel, dedicated in 1991 by the first President Bush.

Laurel Lodge, a "new" facility built in 1972, stood a quarter mile downhill from Aspen, serving as Camp David's site for most official meetings and meals. It included three conference rooms, a spacious dining room and kitchen, with a small presidential office. The former Laurel Lodge, "demoted" and renamed as Holly Cabin, had hosted President Jimmy Carter's Middle Eastern peace negotiations in 1978, landing that year's Nobel Peace Prize for Israeli Prime Minister Menachem Begin.

A military barracks, situated east of present-day Laurel Lodge, housed members of permanent Marine Security Company-Camp David, consisting of one forty-three-member platoon in the president's absence, increased to company strength—three full platoons—when the first family and other guests were present on the property.

Hickory Lodge featured a bowling alley, movie theater, restaurant and bar, game room, library, and the Shangri-La Gift Shop, named for President Franklin Roosevelt's original tag for the retreat. President Dwight Eisenhower had changed the facility's name to "Camp David", simultaneously honoring his father and grandson, who shared that given name.

For more serious recreation, visitors patronized the Wye Oak Fitness Center, featuring a broad range of exercise equipment including cardiovascular machines and free weights for strength training. Treadmills, a basketball court and indoor swimming pool. For those seeking diversion in the great outdoors, Camp David also had a golf course, tennis courts, a skeet-shooting range, bike paths and trails for horseback riding, an outdoor swimming pool and hot tub, a horseshoe pitch and archery range, ski slopes and a skating rink for winter, and bath houses open year-round.

Its large facilities aside, the camp was also sprinkled with individual cabins, small but still luxurious, named for trees including Birch, Cedar, Dogwood, Hawthorn, Linden, Maple, Poplar, Red Oak, Rosebud, Southern Pine, Sycamore, Walnut and Witch Hazel.

How many raiders would it take to seize and hold the whole

shebang? With 129 marines on the ground, plus a nearly equal number of Secret Service and Mossad agents combined, Cody had trouble picturing a mobile strike force entering on foot.

But if they didn't plan to *hold* Camp David, if their plan called for a hit-and-run attack, inflicting maximum casualties in a limited time frame...well, that could be doable, sure.

In fact, it sounded like the kind of mission Cody might have taken gladly, if the roles had been reversed.

Whatever the attackers had in mind, though—and whoever they might be or represent—Cody knew one thing beyond any shadow of a doubt.

They'd come prepared to kill, perhaps to die, taking as many good men and good women with them as they could.

What could he do to stop that, as one man acting alone?

For the first time today, Cody allowed himself a smile.

If any of his foes had seen it, they might well have reconsidered taking on a warrior whose best friends had dubbed him "Suicide".

CHAPTER 8

Camp David Helipad

Nick Blair lay undercover in a copse of trees some twenty yards south of the helipad presently occupied by a Bell UH-1Y Venom helicopter with the U.S. Presidential Seal emblazoned on its fuselage. That symbol was a stick-on, magnetized and easily transferable to any other chopper that might bear the POTUS skyward and thus be designated temporarily as "Marine One".

A lone guard paced around the helipad, wearing the standard camouflage and carrying an M16A4 selective fire assault rifle. At frequent intervals, the sentry raised a walkie-talkie to his lips and muttered something, then waited in vain for a response.

Blair knew he'd wait all night—or rather, for whatever length of time he managed to survive. Sophisticated jamming units had transformed Camp David into a dead zone for radios, computers and cell phones. That jamming would continue while his mission was in progress, with no messages dispatched by any electronic means, and likewise, none received.

That silencer would inevitably raise alarms in Washington and at the USMC base responsible for Camp David's security, but that didn't concern him. By the time the base commander realized that something had gone badly, irretrievably awry, no reinforcements would have access to the helipad, and any troops arriving via highway would be forced to run a lethal gauntlet when they tried to breach the gates.

But first, the UH-1Y Venom chopper had to go.

Some fifty yards beyond the helipad, Blair heard and saw U.S. Marines leaving the long two-story barracks in a rush, all armed with automatic weapons, some still wrestling to button up their uniforms. He didn't have to tell his mercs their job, having rehearsed the drill with them till they were sick of it. Just leave them to it and see how the first hand of this game played out.

The Huey Venom was all his.

Like half the other warriors on his team, Blair carried a Colt Mark 18 CQBR with a 40mm M203 grenade launcher clamped beneath the rifle's barrel. The initials stood for Close Quarter Battle Receiver, referring to a replacement upper receiver for the venerable M4A1 Carbine, reducing barrel length to 10.3 inches and making the CQBR easier to use in and around vehicles or in tight confined spaces. Beyond that, it still fired the same 5.56×45mm NATO rounds from twenty- or thirty-round detachable STANAG magazines, with a full-auto cyclic rate of 900 rounds per minute.

But first, Blair counted on the under-barrel launcher to eliminate one of their major problems.

Lining up his sights while lying prone, he fired a 40mm HE canister into the Venom's cabin windscreen, where it detonated on impact. The force of that explosion touched off twin fuel tanks and split the Huey's fifty-eight-foot fuselage from cockpit to its tail assembly, lighting up the tarmac with a fireball rising close to fifty feet above the shattered aircraft. Fitted out for transportation of executives rather than combat, this particular Venom carried no Hydra 70 unguided rockets, nor were any needed to finish it off.

The shock wave from its instantaneous destruction killed the sentry left to watch the chopper overnight. Its forty-eight-foot rotors, suddenly released like blades from a disintegrating giant fan, spun off in all directions, whickering in flight until two of them met marines advancing on the helipad and cut them down like grass before a power mower. One blade hurtled on to strike the barracks just as more marines emerged, dismembering a few before it came to rest inside the lobby.

After that, it all came down to mopping up.

Blair's mercenaries carried it from there, while he joined in to drop a couple more Camp David guards to demonstrate his own team spirit. When the firing tapered off, the helipad resembled a large outdoor butcher shop, blood-drenched except where flames had vaporized the fluid outpouring of ruptured flesh.

How many dead?

Blair hadn't counted as they fell, but he supposed no more than thirty-odd marines would have been assigned to roving guard duty on any shift. Subtract those missing leathernecks from an ideal company strength of one hundred thirty, and his men taken down 70-odd percent of the retreat's enlisted men at one fell swoop.

And better yet, Blair's 40mm round prevented any rescue flights from landing on Camp David's helipad, the only point of airborne access to its wooded acreage.

Rising from a flattened bed of grass and ferns, he smiled and spoke aloud for the first time since they had breached the compound's outer fence.

"Whoever said no one could crack this joint," Blair said, "he obviously hadn't thought it through."

***

Aspen Lodge

A pair of Secret Service agents stopped him when Cody neared the presidential hideaway. They looked a bit incongruous—a salt-and-pepper team, one white, the other black, in suits and ties— but Cody focused on the weapons they had pointed at him as they ordered him to halt.

The white guy held a KAC SR-16 produced by Knight's Armament Company in Florida, an AR variant carbine Secret Service headquarters had purchased to replace their older M4 carbines in the early 2010s. Chambered for 5.56x45mm NATO cartridges like its parent weapon, the SR-16 fired 750 rounds per minute on full auto, burning through a magazine in less than three seconds.

The rifleman's partner had Cody covered with a Remington Model 870 pump-action shotgun with a thirty-inch barrel and extended magazine holding seven twelve-gauge rounds behind one in the chamber. Cody assumed the shotgun would be loaded with double-aught buckshot, each plastic cartridge containing eight .33-caliber lead projectiles, any one of which could drop a man stone dead.

The rifleman had spotted Cody's "GUEST" tag dangling from his overcoat's lapel but wasn't settling for what could be a cheap and easy means of cover.

"ID," he demanded. "Use your left hand, nice and slow."

Cody was fishing for his wallet when a loud explosion echoed through the woods around them, drawing all eyes toward the compound's heliport and barracks for marines. Before that shockwave had a chance to dissipate, the rattling sound of automatic rifles overtook it, one hellacious firefight joined—and just as quickly muted.

Was that good or bad news?

Cody couldn't guess and put it out of mind, presenting his wallet to the black agent who stepped up to take it, while his partner edged aside and kept Cody framed in his rifle's sights.

"Cody," the second agent read aloud. "I recognize that name. You're on the invitation list."

"And now I need to see the president," Cody replied.

"Why is that?" the rifleman inquired.

"To tell him what I saw and what we're up against," Cody replied. "That racket from the helipad should tell you that it's urgent."

"Maybe the gyrenes have it contained," the shotgunner surmised.

"We can't take that for granted," Cody answered.

"First," the rifleman chimed in, "there's no *we* to it. POTUS and the first lady are under guard by Secret Service personnel. They're not receiving any visitors right now."

"Meaning you've got them stashed downstairs," Cody replied. "I'd say it's fifty-fifty whether that's protection or a death trap."

"We know what we're doing, Mister Cody."

"During motorcades and rallies, maybe on the White House grounds, no doubt. But what you have here is a paramilitary unit coming through the woods. They've breached the fence and now, unless I miss my guess, they've fixed it so that reinforcements can't come in by air. Does that sound like a normal situation to you gentlemen?"

The shotgunner was frowning at him. "I'd say it sounds like you know too goddamned much about what's going on for any so-called guest. What's up with that?"

"How much time do you want to waste chewing the fat?" Cody replied.

"Consider this your entry exam," the Anglo agent countered.

"Fine. I'll give you the short version. Bear in mind that everything you hear is classified and need-to-know."

Starting from there, he told them about Florida, using the sketchiest of language, saying only that he'd been required to help an unnamed member of the first family, heading off what now appeared to be a prelude to the present night's attack. When he was done, the rifleman unclipped a walkie-talkie from his belt and paged someone inside the Aspen Lodge.

Or tried to, anyway.

"Shit! I can't raise anyone," he said.

The shotgunner tried next but had no better luck with his small two-way radio. Next up, they both tried cell phones, all in vain.

"They're jamming," Cody said. "All frequencies."

"How's that?" the shotgunner inquired.

"You missed the memo?" Cody answered. "Anyone can get a multi-function jammer from the Internet today. They run about eight hundred dollars, nothing for a job like this, and cover cell phones, walkies, Blue Tooth, CCTV, Wi-Fi, UHF and VHF, whatever. Bottom line, you can't receive, call out, or keep in touch with any other agents on the property unless you're talking face-to-face, like we are now."

"Mister," the man behind the Remington cautioned, "if this turns out to be a load of crap, I'll put you down without a second thought."

At last we're getting somewhere, Cody thought.

And said, "I wouldn't have it any other way."

✳✳✳

Laurel Lodge

"So, are we safe yet?" Shayna Harwood asked the Secret Service agent standing closest to her in the underground facility to which she and her sister had been marched at double-time, ringed in by men with guns.

"The walls and ceiling are made out of ferroconcrete, reinforced with steel rebars," the agent said. "We have an independent ventilation system, running water, and a backup generator if the power's cut again."

"Sounds like a bomb shelter," Shayna observed.

"In fact, it is," her guard replied. "With all modern conveniences, of course."

"Like cell phones?" Marianna Hardwood asked him, her Nokia smartphone in hand. "Because I'm getting no reception here."

One of the other agents checked his cell and frowned. "Ditto on that," he told the man in charge.

Another pulled a walkie-talkie from beneath his jacket, thumbed down the transmission key, and got only a blast of static for his effort. "Nothing on the radio," he said, unnecessarily.

"Has anybody tried the Wi-Fi?" Shayna asked.

"Checking it now, ma'am," said another of their escorts. Call him Agent No. 3. A moment later he stepped back from the laptop in front of him and said, "No service."

"So, this 'shelter's' looking more like King Tut's tomb right now, minus the scarab beetles," Shayna said.

Agent Rupert Malcolm, heading their security detail, told those around him, "Settle down, please. No one's loving this, but we've got shelter, weapons, food and water. Those are all good things."

"Maybe," said Shayna, "if we're waiting out a siege. How

long did those guys last inside the Alamo?"

"We're not cut off, Miz Harwood," Malcolm answered. "Camp David has one hundred thirty marines on-site, plus forty odd Secret Service personnel and Prime Minister Abramson's Mossad security force. With or without cell phone service, the compound has a helipad for reinforcement and clear access from the highway. There's a naval support facility six miles away to the southeast, plus National Park personnel, Maryland State Police, and officers of the Frederick County Sheriff's Department. Trust me when I say we've got you covered."

Marianna chimed in, asking, "Agent Malcolm, can you tell us anything about what's happening topside? A hint, for starters? Anything at all?"

Malcolm came close to blushing, but beyond that, hung on to his normal cool exterior. "I don't possess that information at the present time, Miz Harwood," he replied.

"So, nothing. Is that it?" she pressed.

"Until we have restored communications—"

"Right. We're screwed."

"Miz Hardwood, please..."

"Have you heard anything about our parents?" Shayna asked him. "Anything at all? I mean, before all your 'secure' communications fell apart?"

"They would have been sequestered automatically," Malcom replied. "That's top priority."

Her grin was wicked as she said, "So, your team's more like Avis, then?"

Malcolm blinked once and said, "Sorry?"

"Come on, Rupe. Avis, right? They ran the same TV ad since the early Sixties. Everybody's heard it one time or another, 'til they changed it up a couple years ago."

"It's not ringing a bell," Malcom confessed.

Shayna put on the sing-song tone of a TV commercial. "We're Number 2, so we try harder. Right? Still nothing?"

Agent Malcolm concentrated on his poker face and glanced at Marianna, obviously thinking, *Can't you bring this kid under control?*

And Marianna's shrug replied, *Good luck with that.*

The muffled sound of an explosion, well removed from the vicinity and muffled by the thick walls of their buried sanctuary, brought a halt to conversation for the moment. Malcolm and another agent tried their cell phones once again but still found themselves without service.

"What could black us out like this?" asked Marianna. "I mean, with the power from the backup generator, what's up with the silent treatment?"

Malcom seemed to have a notion, but he kept it to himself, maybe to keep from worrying the Harwood sisters any further. "Hard to say," he finally allowed.

"And that explosion?" Shayna challenged him. "That can't be good, right?"

Malcom stalled some more, then said, "I really—"

"Couldn't say," the sisters interrupted him as one, almost enough to put a fleeting grin on Marianna's face.

That didn't last, though. Cut off from her parents, from

her brother and his family, in fact the whole damned world at large, fear and frustration crowded out the small respite of mirth. It had been years since she'd felt anything like this, and even then—a panicky weekend in college, when she'd feared she might be pregnant—there had been no threat of death involved.

And truth be told, she wasn't sure now, whether she should scream in anger or break down and cry.

✱✱✱

Approaching Holly Cabin

"How come we get sent after the Jews?" Fabius Worthy asked. There was a hint of Brooklyn in his voice, most likely Bedford–Stuyvesant.

"Who cares?" Tom Altman countered. "We're a part of it. We're getting paid. No matter how you slice it, that's what counts."

"Thing is, I like to play first-string, you know?" Worthy replied. "I don't like messing with this JV shit."

"What are you, still in high school?"

"No, man, that's my point. I've paid my dues and then some. Anybody's gonna cap the Main Man, I want to be in on it."

"Too bad we drew the short straw, then," said Altman. "If it helps, this Abramson's the top man in Israel."

"BFD, yo. We're still getting leftovers."

"I take it that you've never squared off the Mossad."

"Not yet," Worthy admitted.

"So, don't talk about 'em till you have. They're all ex-IDF, same guys who've been out in the desert kicking ass since 1948."

"Correction," Worthy countered. "Kicking *Arab* asses. That's like ripping off a baby's pacifier, yo. I smoked fifty or sixty of 'em, doing four tours in the sand for Uncle Sugar."

Altman raised a cautionary finger to his lips and silenced Worthy. They had almost reached the cabin labeled "Holly" on their topo maps of Camp David, and he was in no mood for telegraphing any punches to the guards in residence.

Altman never felt wholly at ease with Worthy, never mind that they were both Americans. Too many obstacles stood in between them, starting out with race, then piling on a native Mississippian teamed with a guy from Gotham. Add to that the never-ending rivalry of Army versus navy, and their very different approaches to combat. With Delta Force, Altman was often in the thick of it, on search-and-rescue missions, last-ditch holding actions and the like. Worthy had done his tours as a designated marksman—what the service used to call a sniper in the good old days, before the Soviets somehow coopted "sniper" and that term fell out of favor in the so-called Free World.

Altman scorned P.C. semantic bullshit, as when trash collectors made the leap to being "sanitary engineers" and janitors became "custodians".

To hell with that.

"I see it, yo," Worthy advised, and pointed toward a structure just becoming visible.

"So that's a cabin," Altman groused, remembering the shack his old man used for hunting weekends in Neshoba County, with no running water and a shithouse out in back.

"That's how the other half camps out, yo. Make you wanna try it on for size, like?"

"NFW," Altman replied.

No freaking way.

"I feel you. Now, what?"

"Take 'em out," Altman reminded him of Nick Blair's order.

"Yeah, but *how,* yo?"

"You've got the PSG1. Cover me while I move up and have a look-see."

"What about CCTV?"

"It's covered, Fab. Don't tell me you forgot about the jammer."

"Ain't forgot nothing," Worthy replied. "Can't say I trust it, though."

"Just keep your eye glued to that Hensoldt," Altman said, referring to the PSG1 rifle's Hensoldt ZF 6×42 telescopic sight with illuminated reticle, manufactured in Upper Bavaria. "And make damned sure you don't shoot me by accident."

"No sweat," Worthy replied, grinning. "I never wasted anyone by accident."

"Okay, then."

Taking Worthy at his word, Altman crept forward, carrying his Mark 18 CQBR, its safety off, the fire selector set for three-round bursts, his index finger still outside the rifle's trigger guard.

When he'd covered half the distance without drawing fire or sounding an alarm, Altman picked up his pace, still being careful where he set his feet to keep from making an unnecessary racket.

Lots of people think the woods and jungles of the world are quiet after nightfall, but experience he'd gained while hunting deer, wild hogs and men had taught Altman that nothing could be further from the truth. Figure on breezes blowing every which way, frogs and insects raising hell, with wildlife of all sizes scuttling all around in search of food, water, maybe a willing mate.

The woods were noisy, man, and jungles were the worst, with apes, big cats and night birds thrown into the mix.

The trick of creeping up on someone didn't like in being silent. Rather, it required an adaptation to the other sounds of Nature that provided background music to a stalk and kill.

And Thomas Altman was a master at his craft.

✻✻✻

Rosebud Cabin

"What do you mean, 'no contact' with the Aspen Lodge?" asked Gary Harwood.

Secret Service Agent Patrick Murphy, chief of Gary's personal security detail, was somewhere in his early fifties but looked older. When he spoke, his voice conveyed a hint of sandpaper, likely from smoking more than anybody should.

"It means exactly what I told you, Mister Harwood. WE have temporarily lost contact with the president's detail by cell or radio."

"Just Aspen Lodge?"

"No, sir. There seems to be a problem with communication in the compound generally."

"What could cause that?" Greta Harwood asked, holding their three-year-old daughter balanced against her right hip.

"Ma'am," Murphy replied, "I can't explain that previously. Any one of half a dozen things could be responsible."

"Such as?" she prodded him.

"Might be the weather, but that seems unlikely. If I had to guess, I'd say some kind of outside interference. An unknown disturbance in the atmosphere, perhaps, or trouble with the cell towers nearby."

"That shouldn't cut the walkie-talkies out," Gary reminded him.

"No, sir. But I was asked to speculate, as you'll recall."

"So, what about an EMP?" the president's son asked.

An electromagnetic pulse, aka a transient electromagnetic disturbance, is a short burst of electromagnetic energy that may disrupt communications, short out circuits, wipe computer hard drives clean—the list went on and on. EMPs may be of natural origin, spawned by lightning or solar flares, while others were manmade, ranging from electrostatic discharge and switching actions of electrical circuits to energy emitted from a nuclear explosion.

Bottom line: whatever cause was deemed responsible the net results were bad.

"I doubt that it would be an EMP, sir," Murphy said.

"Why not?" asked Greta. "We all heard that blast a few minutes ago."

"Yes, ma'am, but a normal explosion—"

"Normal?" Gary interrupted him. "What could be normal about an explosion at Camp David?"

"What I meant, sir—"

"How about a landline?" Greta challenged. "I know they're old-fashioned, but they work even when the power's blacked out, right?"

"Affirmative," said Murphy.

"Well, then?"

"Ma'am, the old landlines around the compound were removed nearly two years ago."

"Removed? For God's sake, why?"

"By presidential order, ma'am."

That silenced any further questions for a moment, until Tina chirped, "Where's Paw Paw?"

Greta gave the child a gentle bounce and said, "Baby, we've got a problem with the phones right now. We're working on it."

"Can't we just go see him?"

From the mouths of babes, thought Gary Harwood. And he told Murphy, "That doesn't sound half-bad to me."

"Sir," Murphy said, "I've already explained—"

"That we're stuck here, can't speak to anyone outside, etcetera. What *can* we do, then, Agent Murphy?"

"Well…it runs against the standard Service protocol…"

"We're listening."

"In an emergency, I am empowered to dispatch one member of my team, someone on the outside, if it's feasible."

"Now, that sounds like a plan," the first son said.

"But as I said—"

"Your protocol. I understand that, Agent Murphy. But the only other choice we have is sitting here and doing nothing. In my world, it's sometimes easier to ask forgiveness than obtain permission. And in this case, when there's no one you can ask for God knows how long…"

"Right. Okay," Murphy conceded. Turning toward his mini-squad of four agents, clustered around the basement stairs, he called out, "Jeff! Step over here a second, son."

Agent Jeffrey Schumacher stepped forward, trying hard to minimize the Uzi submachine gun dangling from his right hand.

"Yes, sir?"

"You ever play 'go fetch'," Murphy inquired.

"Sir?"

"You're my volunteer, son. I need you to go upstairs and make your way to Aspen Lodge. Be careful, right? And if there's any reason you can't make it, come back double quick and fill me in."

Schumacher glanced from Murphy to the Harwoods watching him, and nodded. "Yes, sir. On my way, sir."

"And if you run into opposition, son, remember that you

have the green light. Got it?"

"Yes, sir!"

"On your way, then. Make me proud."

"I'll do my best, sir."

Gary Harwood watched the young man with his SMG retrace the path they'd followed coming downstairs to the basement shelter, until he vanished from sight. A second agent, trailing him, secured and double locked the access door that was intended to stop bullets and repel explosive shrapnel.

Gary's engineering skills did not extend to judging whether that door would protect them in the case of an attack or not, but he was sure of one thing beyond any doubt.

Their best chance of survival lay in getting out, as far away from Camp David as possible.

***

Laurel Lodge

"Where are you going, Sara?" DCI Whit Jones demanded, rising to his feet from an extravagantly padded armchair, trying not to spill his whisky sour.

"Out to see what's happening," Sara Durell replied, not turning back to face him, briskly striding toward the basement staircase and its intervening fireproof door.

"To do what?" Jones inquired, not quite sarcastically. "You can't hope to accomplish anything—"

"Cooling my heels down here," she finished for him, still

without a backward glance.

A Secret Service agent with a crew cut short enough to bare his scalp was on the door, a Micro UZI submachine gun looking like a child's toy in his hands. As she approached, he took a single forward step to block her path.

"Get real," she cautioned him. "That is the worst mistake that you could make right now."

"Ma'am..."

Sara was deciding where to kick him, and how hard, Jones spoke up again, behind her, saying, "Sara, I forbid this reckless course of action."

"You *forbid* it?" Sara felt the acid of frustration etching a crooked smile across her face as she turned back to focus on the DCI. "Is that what you just said?"

"If you won't stand down voluntarily," Jones said, "then yes, I do forbid it. Call it a direct order. You *will not* leave this shelter under pain of being severed from the Company."

Her own laughter at that surprised Sara. "I hear you, Whit. That doesn't mean I'm listening, much less obeying you."

"Sara—"

"Stop talking," she advised him. "Fire me if you want to, if you ever make it out of here alive. Or I can text my resignation to you now, before I go." Her smile widened a bit before she added, "Oh, that's right. I can't text anything because the goddamned phones are out, along with radios, Wi-Fi, and any other method of communication you can name. So, why don't we go old school, then. I quit."

For reasons that she couldn't grasp, that brought the White

House chief of staff up from the love seat where he'd been reclining with a beer bottle in hand. James Corbett's tone was almost pleading when he said, "Can we all take a breather now, for just a second? Everyone calm down, all right? We've got a situation, and the best thing we can do right now is—"

"Let me guess," she interrupted him. "Were you about to say, 'Do squat about it?' Maybe bigger, highfalutin words to that effect? Why don't you save it for the cameras, assuming that you ever see another one?"

Red-faced, Corbett blustered, "Now, listen here—"

"No, thanks. I'm all done listening. It's time to *do something* besides just hiding underground like prairie dogs."

Sara turned back to face the frowning Secret Service agent, reinforced within the past few seconds by a second operative who apparently believed shaving his head made him resemble handsome "Agent 47" from the movie *Hitman*.

He was wrong.

"Okay, boys," Sara told them both. "There are two ways for us to do this. Number one, you step aside and lock the door behind him to protect these *gentlemen*. Or, number two, you shoot me. That's what it will take to stop me going through that door behind you."

"Ma'am..."

"Tick-tock," she said. "I'm tired of waiting, fellas."

Almost without planning it, she eased into a loose Krav Maga "contact combat" stance, prepared to launch herself at one or both with no holds barred.

Behind her, Whit Jones heaved a sigh and told the agents, "Let her pass, for God's sake."

When the agent with the Uzi twitched his eyes toward Jones, Sara decided she would drop him first, retrieve his little SMG, then deal with his backup.

"Sir," Uzi Man started to say, but DCI Jones cut him off.

"I'm telling you to let her pass. You both know me, and I am speaking with the full authority of Langley."

"I'll see that and raise you the White House," Corbett added, sounding whipped. "Just stop this. Now!"

With visible reluctance, the two agents facing Sara stood aside. She thought about plucking the Mini Uzi from her first antagonist's big hands but let it slide.

The problem with Camp David wasn't lack of guns, but rather knowing how and where to find them stashed. Climbing the concrete access stairs, she heard the fire door close behind her, its locks snapping into place with grim finality, a sound like breaking bones.

Guns first, and then she had to find out what was happening above ground in the presidential getaway. Discover that and put a stop to it by any means required.

With any luck she'd find Jack Cody and he'd help her.

That is, if no one had killed him yet.

✳✳✳

Baltimore

Seventy miles and change southwestward from Camp David, Thaddeus Resnikoff paced the living room of his penthouse hotel suite, ignoring his picture window's panoramic view of the Patapsco River, the National Aquarium, and the American Visionary Art Museum.

There was so much to see and do in Baltimore, but none of it meant anything to Resnikoff just now.

The cognac snifter in his left hand was his fourth since midnight, yet he barely felt a hint of impact from the smooth Courvoisier he had consumed so far.

Courvoisier XO, for "extra old", advertised as "the cognac of Napoléon" since 1812, was the only cognac Resnikoff drank, and it normally gave him a warm mellow feeling inside. Tonight, however, the arms dealer thought he could have downed a liter bottle, maybe more, without feeling a thing.

The coup of a lifetime was under way, barely an hour and a quarter's drive from where he stood surveying Baltimore by night, and waiting for the sun to rise on a new day. If it succeeded—if Nick Blair could pull it off—then Resnikoff, already rich, would be a man of wealth beyond his wildest dreams.

But if it failed, if Blair and his small army failed, there would be hell to pay.

That Resnikoff did not believe that he would be suspected, much less charged with any crime. He certainly would not be tried, much less convicted, for the countless felonies he'd set in motion to enrich himself.

Unbidden, Resnikoff began to list those crimes. He started at the top—or bottom, all depending on your point of view—with federal offenses that could land a convict on death row.

He could not be charged with treason, since that statute only applied to persons "owing allegiance to the United States". As a non-citizen, he was exempt from that count, and was likewise clear on espionage, since he'd made no effort to collect or transmit any classified material. Ditto for piracy, large-scale drug trafficking, or the attempted murder of a witness, juror, or court officer in certain specified cases, such as racketeering.

In fact, the only federal prison inmates currently facing execution—sixty-three of them, mostly confined to the U.S. penitentiary at Terre Haute, Indiana—stood convicted of aggravated murder. That heading alone included thirty separate crimes rating lethal injection, and while some of those clearly would not apply to Resnikoff, he would be deemed guilty under at least ??? provisions of the U.S. Code, Title 18.

Whether he won or lost tonight, Resnikoff faced death for killing or conspiring to kill a sitting president and members of his staff, causing death by use of an illegal firearm or explosive, murder committed while lying in wait, possibly murder by arson, and murder deemed "willful, deliberate, malicious, and premeditated".

Whatever else happened tonight, no one could rationally claim it was an accident.

Of course, the feds would have to capture Resnikoff before they could convict him, and even if sentenced to death, the odds of him finally riding a gurney were slight. During the present century so far, only three federal inmates had been executed: Oklahoma City bomber Timothy McVeigh, whose appeals spanned six years; marijuana smuggler Juan Raul

Garza, convicted of killing eight cohorts or rivals (eight years on appeal); and ex-soldier Louis Jones Jr., for the kidnapping and rape slaying of an army intelligence trainee (another eight years on appeal).

Furthermore, while Terre Haute's death row was chock-full, no other inmates had been put to death since March 2003, swiftly approaching two decades.

But death, per se, was not the problem. Truth be told, Thad Resnikoff would *rather* die than be confined behind stone walls for life without parole. If it came down to that, he knew at least a hundred fairly simple ways to kill himself and thereby cheat the executioners.

Besides, he thought there was a good chance that his plot would be successful. He was not dismayed by lack of news broadcast so far. By severing communications from Camp David, Blair had stalled reporting on the raid, also delaying armed response by any agency empowered to react—the U.S. military, FBI and Secret Service, U.S. Marshals, take your pick.

Success was still within Resnikoff's grasp, and if he failed, the preparations for escape had been completed in advance.

Now, all he had to do was wait.

✳✳✳

Aspen Lodge

Hans Behrens was proud to have drawn the raid's plum assignment, storming the presidential mansion at Camp David with Adriaan Coetzee to take out the first family.

It wouldn't be easy, of course, but what worthwhile goal ever was?

In Nick Blair's place, Behrens supposed he might have sent more men to do the job, but with a force so small, spread out over the wooded compound and assaulting multiple high-value targets simultaneously, corners were inevitably cut.

And Behrens had no doubt that he could pull it off, together with his comrade from Johannesburg.

They'd bonded during training for this mission, starting off from similar backgrounds. Like most soldiers in Germany, Behrens stood somewhere to the right of Genghis Khan politically, and Coetzee was the next best thing to a soulmate without trespassing on gay territory.

Germany and the Republic of South Africa had much in common, stretching back through history, despite the fact that modern leaders in both countries had betrayed the nations that they served. South Africa's original white settlers were the Boers—Dutch for "farmers"—who had fought tenaciously against the Brits for liberty. They'd lost those wars but ultimately won the peace that followed, establishing a system of apartheid—"apartness", meaning rigid racial segregation—that was not so different from Adolf Hitler's statutes penalizing Jews. In fact, the National Party, apartheid's founders, was led by Third Reich sympathizers who adopted their racial policies in equal measure from Canada's Indian Act of 1876 and the Nuremberg Laws of 1935.

You might have said that Behrens and Coetzee were kinsmen of a sort, their outlook on the world spanning five generations of racist war mongers—or sterling patriots, depending on how people chose to look at it. No matter that their two respective countries had been weakened and subverted by a host of dusky interlopers and politicians obsessed with "political correctness". Both men knew what they were fighting for, and money didn't cover all of it by any means.

That said, of course, they still expected to be paid—and handsomely—for working at the only job they'd ever loved.

As they approached the Aspen Lodge, Behrens saw two men dressed in suits and overcoats, topped off by hats with ear flaps, standing guard in plain view on the mansion's lower terrace. Both were armed, one with a shotgun and the other with some version of the M16 assault rifle, presumably the SR-16 carbines issued as standard by the U.S. Secret Service since 2006.

Guns were a mercenary's business, and both warriors knew them inside-out.

A cautious circuit of the lodge had shown them no more outer guards, although Behrens was confident there would be plenty more inside. At least a dozen normally watched over the first family, and Behrens didn't relish the idea of stalking them throughout the lodge's many rooms.

A better plan was to eliminate the pair out front, then use explosives to precipitate a rout from Aspen Lodge into the night, where guards and those whom they were paid to safeguard would be easy marks for Behrens with his MP5 and Coetzee's Mark 18 CQBR.

To breach the lodge, they carried blocks of C-4 plastique, timer fuses, and assorted hand grenades: M68 fragmentation, M15 white phosphorous (or "willie peter"), and M14 thermite incendiaries. They hadn't bothered packing in M116/A1 "flash-crash" grenades, gas canisters, or any of the other "less lethal" grenades available on the black market.

Why should they, when none of their targets were expected to survive?

Lying together in deep shadows, eyeballing the lodge's visible lookouts, Coetzee asked Behrens, "Do you want to take them, or shall I?"

"My pleasure," Behrens said, and meant it, sighting down the barrel of his MP5SD, the model with an integrated sound suppressor ranked by experts as the most effective firearms "silencer" on Earth. The range was fifty feet or slightly less, no challenge whatsoever for his SMG.

The MP5's selector switch has five settings: safe, semi-automatic, two- or three-round bursts, and full auto. For this job, Behrens set his on the red numeral "2" and finished lining up his shot.

A perfect double double-tap.

***

Cody had no trouble locating the Aspen Lodge's armory. He'd asked directions to it on arrival, and he went directly to it now, before considering a visit to the president and his first lady huddled in their shelter underground.

Considering the Secret Service guards stationed at Aspen Lodge, Cody wasn't surprised to find the armory depleted now, but he still found an SR-16 carbine for himself and backed it up with a stubby MP5K submachine gun—"K" stood for the German *kurz*, or "short", although the smaller weapon still maintained its parent's fearsome firepower.

Finally, he retrieved a canvas shoulder bag from the gun closet, stuffing it with extra magazines for both his automatic weapons before turning toward the kitchen and its staircase leading to the bunker down below. An agent on the reinforced steel door eyeballed the guns Cody was carrying and double-checked his photo I.D. before passing him through.

No call downstairs, of course. The compound's link to anyone outside—or even between structures on the grounds— was still blacked out and likely to remain that way.

Another agent on the door downstairs repeated that procedure, following the printed rules and wasting precious time. He muttered something about taking Cody's weapons while he went inside the presidential shelter, then thought better of it after Cody told him he should ask The Man inside and take his orders from the top.

Now, standing once again in Martin Harwood's presence, with his wife Pavlina and another group of Secret Service agents looking on, Cody laid out his plan as quickly and concisely as he could.

When he was done, the POTUS said, "I like your spirit, Jack. But do you think it's helpful, going off alone like that? I mean, we have the Secret Service and a company of highly trained marines, plus hard-core agents from Mossad guarding Israel's prime minister."

"Excuse me, Mister President," Cody interrupted. "I wouldn't be counting on the site's marines if I were you."

"And why not, may I ask?"

"On my way over here," Cody replied, "I heard a firefight going on outside their barracks. That was after an explosion on the helipad. Long story short, if you've got any leathernecks still living on the property, my guess is that they're hurting, and they won't be getting reinforced or resupplied by air."

The president turned to an agent standing at his left elbow, demanding, "Is this true?"

The agent gave a shrug and said, "I'm sorry, Mister President, but while we're cut off from communicating with the rest of the compound, much less the outside world...I really couldn't say."

"Goddamn it!" Harwood scowled. "All right, then, Jack. What do you have in mind specifically?"

"I couldn't give it to you point by point, sir. Once I'm back outside, engage the enemy wherever I can find them, take them out, and go from there. I'm improvising. Playing it by ear."

"I see." The president looked skeptical. "You'll understand if I feel something less than confident about a plan so ill-defined."

"Frankly, I'd think you'd lost your marbles if you didn't, Mister President. I can't stand here and promise you success, when I have no idea how many infiltrators are involved or where they've been deployed."

"You haven't mentioned how they're armed," Harwood observed.

"On that score," Cody said, "I take for granted that they came prepared with tools to do whatever job they've got in mind. Somebody spent a bundle on this deal, which tells me someone, somewhere, plans to get a good rate of return."

The president let that sink in, then nodded slowly.

"Right, then. Since I haven't lost my marbles, as you put it, go ahead and do what you do best."

Those words were barely out before a loud explosion rocked the lodge and killed its generator, blacking out the big house from its attic to the basement hideaway.

CHAPTER 9

Approaching the Barracks

Colonel Owen "Blades" McConnell sniffed the chill night wind, immediately struck by the grim stench of death and burning helicopter fuel.

He was acquainted with both odors, from his combat flights during three Middle Eastern wars, and while he'd hope each time that it would be the *last* time, that had not worked out for him so far.

From Operation Desert Storm, on to Afghanistan and then back to Iraq, whether a war was formally declared or written off as a "police action", men died and choppers burned. McConnell had flown into hostile fire repeatedly, extracting wounded warriors and the ones who hadn't lived to hear his helicopter coming for them, and he had been decorated with the Navy Cross, Navy Distinguished Service Medal, Navy and Marine Corps Commendation Medal and Achievement Medal, plus five Purple Hearts for combat wounds of differing severity—the worst of had laid him up in hospital for seven dreary weeks.

Along the way he'd killed men, too, flying both the Bell UH-1Y Venom and AH-1Z Viper light attack choppers, strafing enemy positions of motorized columns with 20mm Gatling canons, 70mm Hydra rockets and next-generation APKWS missiles (short for "*A*dvanced *P*recision *K*ill *W*eapon *S*ystem"), and AGM-114 Hellfire air-to-surface missiles. Whenever some stuffed shirt asked how he felt about that— likely wondering if he would boast or weep—McConnell always answered that he felt no way about it.

Total strangers sometimes tried to kill him, and he'd beat them to the punch.

If anything, Blades felt relieved.

Right now, he was beyond his normal element, not soaring over godforsaken killing grounds, but moving through the blacked-out woods on foot, wearing his coat collar turned up around the lower portion of his face to keep from trailing ghostly plumes with every breath.

His enemies—more strangers to McConnell—were somewhere around him in those woods, but so far, he had not run into them. His target was the USMC barracks and its helipad, where he'd last seen his UH-1Y Venom, tagged for the duration as "Marine Two". And every step he took increased a sense of dark foreboding that he couldn't shake.

Upon departure from D.C., McConnell had been tempted to question the designation of his chopper. "Marine One" was meant to haul the president around, and while it had developed a hydraulic leak, Blades couldn't fathom why the officer in charge of naming aircraft had decided to call the replacement Venom "Marine Two". According to Marine Corps regulations, that title applied to any aircraft used by the Vice President of the United States, and not by his immediate superior.

Instead of asking, though—and pissing someone off to no result—McConnell had kept quiet. Now he wondered if that hiccup had foretold a chain of most unfortunate events that wasn't finished yet.

Dumb superstition, anyway. And yet...

McConnell saw the flames before he reached the helipad, the close-up reek of spilled and burnt-off fuel almost enough to gag him. Seconds later, he could see the chopper was demolished, its remains still smoking from the blast that had destroyed it.

By its fading firelight, he could also see the scattered, crumpled bodies of marines in uniform, their rifles strewn around the barracks law and helipad's blacktop before they even had a chance at target acquisition.

It had been a massacre.

He couldn't tell how many adversaries were involved in the ambush. None lingered at the smoking battleground, but Blades picked out the gleam of spent brass strewn about the grass and weeds from which they'd opened fire upon the startled leathernecks.

So many dead to start with, but that still wasn't the worst of it.

By taking out "Marine Two" with explosives—likely a grenade launcher, he guessed—the raiders had blocked access to the compound's vital helipad.

Which meant no reinforcements landing at Camp David to relieve the siege.

Topography ruled out setting a chopper down at any other site within the grounds, so pilots would be forced to hover while their passengers rappelled to earth, exposed to hostile fire the whole way down.

Both dangling warriors and their airships would be easy marks for gunmen on the ground.

McConnell backed away, mouthing a silent curse, and started back toward Red Oak Cabin, where he'd started out. He needed to collect his thoughts and strategize.

Unless some bastard picked him off en route.

✳✳✳

Aspen Lodge

Jack Cody bummed a Maglite Mini PRO LED two-cell flash-light from one of the Secret Service agents stuck below ground with the POTUS and his first lady, making his cautious way upstairs and out onto the first floor of the lodge. More agents met him there and waved him toward the nearest exit, one guy trailing him to double lock the outer door once Cody had passed through it.

As he stepped into the chilled night air, Cody knew he was abandoning the safety of four walls in favor of a manhunt through the midnight forest, over unfamiliar ground he had not scouted thoroughly by daylight.

And why would he have bothered? Who knew that a strike force was descending on Camp David? Who in his right mind even would have considered it?

On most assignments Cody handled for the CIA, he started with a goal and a description of his enemies—if not their given names, at least an ideology they claimed to follow, possibly a group affiliation to define their goals.

Tonight, he would be starting off with zero information, hampered by that ignorance.

Identities? Forget about it.

Aims? Perhaps to harm the President of the United States or members of his family—although, with Jairus Abramson in residence, it could turn out to be a Middle Eastern thing, continuation of the endless struggle between Jews and Arabs that had raged since 1948 or even earlier, beginning with the paramilitary Zionist rebellion against Britain in what once was known as Mandatory Palestine. That pushed it back to 1921, nearly a century of endless war, so many homicides and other acts of terrorism piling up that few modern observers could remember how it all began.

To hell with all of that, thought Cody.

He was interested only in the here and now. To beat the adversaries who'd invaded Camp David and seemed well on their way to overrunning it, he had to put himself inside their minds, try to determine real-world motives, and then interpose himself between the enemy and those it was his duty to defend.

But first, before all that, he had to exit Aspen Lodge, confront the man or men who'd set off the explosive charge just moments earlier—and having found them, put them down.

Simple? Not even close.

Moving through darkness, from the vacant kitchen to the spacious living room, he saw no damage wrought by the explosive charge that had blacked out the lodge. He caught the too-familiar almond scent of C-4 plastique, wafting through the lodge from somewhere relatively close at hand. That led him to the lower terrace, moving stealthily toward the adjacent shed where tools were kept, and where the lodge's backup generator had been housed.

Nearing that target, Cody didn't use his Maglite Mini, careful not to give himself away. He didn't need the flashlight, finally, to tell the lodge's shed had been demolished by the blast that left its occupants stranded in stygian darkness.

But where were the invaders who had touched it off?

It made no sense for them to hit and run, without trying to reach the POTUS and his wife inside. Unless they were primary targets, why even attack the Aspen Lodge at all?

Before his mind could grapple with that question, muzzle flashes blazed in front of him and Cody dropped, hearing the hiss of bullets passing overhead.

✳✳✳

Dogwood Cabin

Sara Durell had cadged an SR-16 carbine and a standard-issue SIG Sauer P229 semiauto pistol from the Secret Service backup stash before she ventured out of Dogwood Cabin to explore Camp David's nightscape.

The P229 was chambered for .357 SIG rounds, a rimless bottleneck cartridge derived from the 10mm Auto cartridge introduced in 1983. The SIG's projectile was smaller in diameter than the 10mm's—.35 caliber versus .40—and its case was shorter, but the slugs traveled at 1,450 feet per second, faster than the 10mm's 1,300, enhancing penetration and knockdown power. The pistol weighed two pounds against the larger autoloader's thirty-eight ounces, thus being easier to carry and deploy in combat.

Overall, both borrowed weapons were manstoppers.

All that Sara needed now were enemies to stop.

But where in hell were they?

The knowledge that they might be *any*where and getting up to damned near anything gave Sara pause, but she had no spare time to waste on angst and second thoughts. She had a dirty job to do—maybe her last for Langley, even if she came out on the other end of it alive—and at the moment she had no clear thoughts on where to start.

With the marines on site, perhaps?

Why not?

She started hiking toward their barracks and the nearby helipad, hoping to meet some of the camp's defenders while en route. Instead, when she was roughly halfway to her destination, Sara started smelling smoke and seeing firelight through the trees. Accordingly, she slowed her pace and kept a firm grip on her carbine, ready to defend herself at any second.

When she heard someone approaching in the opposite direction, moving stealthily but short of silently, she stopped dead in her tracks and crouched behind a large oak tree, the SR-16 at her shoulder, sighting down its barrel into darkness.

As a solitary man came into view, Sara called out to him, "That's far enough! Show me your hands!"

"Sara?" the voice came back to her, not quite a whisper. "Is that you?"

"Owen?"

"I'm coming in," McConnell answered. "Don't waste me if you can help it."

"Come ahead."

When he was next to her, he asked Sara, "Where are you headed?"

"To the barracks and the helipad, for help."

"Too late," Blades said. "I've just been there."

"Trouble?"

"In spades. Somebody blew my chopper up, and now the helipad's impassable, but that isn't the worst of it."

She saw where he was headed and anticipated his next words. "The guards are out of it?"

McConnell nodded. "Most of them," he said. "There should still be a few scattered around the compound on patrol, but the majority, along with their commanding officer, were ambushed while responding to the Huey going up in smoke."

"Survivors?" Sara pressed him.

"None that I saw."

"Jesus, Blades."

"I know."

"And they were taken down with what?"

"Full auto weapons, varied calibers according to the brass they left behind. At least two different calibers, nine-millimeter Parabellum and 5.56 NATO. Beyond that, I couldn't begin to guess how many shooters were involved."

Before Sara could answer that, both of them heard a thunderous explosion north by northwest from the spot they occupied.

"That sounds like Aspen Lodge," Sara surmised.

"The president," McConnell said.

"I'm heading that way, then," Sara replied.

"I'll tag along if you don't mind, but I'm not packing."

Sara reached inside her coat, retrieved the P229 and handed it to Blades, with a pair of extra magazines. "You are now, Colonel."

"I'd rather have a SuperCobra or a Viper, but I'll take what I can get."

"One other thing," Sara advised. "Watch out for Cody on the way."

"Where's he supposed to be?" McConnell asked.

" 'Supposed to be' doesn't mean much to Jack," she said. "Whatever's going on tonight, we can expect him to be in the thick of it."

✳✳✳

Holly Cabin

"I don't like being trapped here like a monkey in a box," Jairus Abramson told Captain Naftali Sharett of Mossad.

"My only job is to ensure that you are safe, Prime Minister," Sharett replied. "Please try to think of it as kept secure, not trapped."

"How can I be secure when we can't see outside? Camp David is supposed to be secure against attack from any quarter, but it's been invaded. From what little we can hear I'd wager the attackers have the upper hand."

"It would require a regiment to seize and hold the property, Prime Minister. The mere logistics are prohibitive."

"And yet it's happening. Can we at least agree on that much, Captain?"

Sharett bobbed his head, a rueful nod of acquiescence. "Yes, sir. But we have a defensible position, weapons to repel attackers. Going out to face them in the night can only make the problem worse."

"Or is it worse to wait and be surrounded in a pit below ground?" Abramson challenged the man assigned to keep him breathing through this visit to the States.

"Prime Minister—"

"If we are cut off and surrounded, Captain, then we shall be at their mercy. They can burn the cabin down around our ears or raze it with explosives. After that, how long before they trace the bunker's ventilation system, introducing gas or an inflammable accelerant? Do you prefer choking on poisoned fumes, as if we'd traveled back in time to Auschwitz, or incinerated in our crematorium below ground?"

"Sir, what would we possibly achieve by going out to meet the enemy, with no idea how many of them there may be or how they are equipped?"

"Captain," the PM said, "only a fool believes that he is truly safe behind closed doors and windows with the blinds pulled down. I understand that you have fought our nation's foes in Gaza?"

"Yes, Prime Minister."

"From my experience at war, before your time, I know that some peasants hope to find sanctuary in their humble dwellings, thinking that the tide of battle will not carry them away if they conceal themselves. Almost inevitably, they are wrong. Walls may stop small arms bullets, but explosives bring them down and bury those inside, or fire and smoke asphyxiate them, cringing in their closets or beneath their beds."

"Sir, this bunker—"

"Was built to shelter occupants from most explosions, even possibly a nuclear airburst. But what of *afterward,* Captain? When is it safe to finally emerge? Without communication, how are we to know? Will the destruction wreaked upon us even make it worthwhile to investigate?"

"Prime Minister—"

But Abramson still was not finished. "Captain, do you know the ritual of Groundhog Day in the United States?"

"Something about a rodent who supposedly predicts the

weather, sir?"

"Indeed. A relative of squirrels and marmots. One small town in Pennsylvania reveres a groundhog known as Philip, I believe. According to a local superstition, each year since the latter 1880s, residents observe the creature's burrow on a certain day in February and expect the rodent to emerge. If 'Phil' beholds his shadow and retreats, it is supposed to mean winter will last another six weeks. If the rodent sees no shadow, it predicts an early spring."

"Ridiculous," Sharett replied. "What animal besides a tortoise lives more than hundred years?"

"Of course, it is ridiculous," said Abramson. "No one outside of an asylum would believe it, but the small town's merchants bank on tourism and use the celebration as a good excuse for swilling lager."

"Sir, I fail to see—"

"We are not groundhogs," interrupted Abramson. "We do not base our life-and-death decisions on things that we fail to see outside. To know what's happening around us, we must look, listen, and learn."

"Prime Minister, my one and only order is to keep you safe."

"To which end, I suppose, you must protect me from myself?"

"It was not phrased to me that way, sir."

"But you understood it all the same. Now tell me, Captain, as prime minister, which member of our government outranks me?"

Grudgingly, Sharett replied, "None, sir."

"Exactly right."

Under their homeland's constitution, dubbed the Basic Laws of Israel, the prime minister was head of government and chief executive. Granted, the nation is a republic, whose voters also elected a president as head of state, but the president's powers are largely ceremonial, while prime ministers hold the real power, including deployment of troops against Israeli's hostile neighbors.

And short of the Knesset passing a vote of "no confidence", no subordinate in government outranked the elected PM.

"Now that we've established that," said Abramson, "what is your first duty, Captain?"

"To follow orders as required."

"Now that we've settled that, here's what you need to do."

***

Aspen Lodge

Jack Cody mouthed a silent curse as he came under hostile fire. He'd ducked in time to save himself from injury, but simply hiding wouldn't cut it when the POTUS and first lady were holed up downstairs, cornered and waiting for their would-be killers to close in.

The raiders had been smart enough to separate after they blew the lodge's backup generator, and they had Cody in a crossfire now, firing coordinated alternating bursts to keep his head down while they jockeyed for position in the dark.

They were adept, well-trained—but not invisible.

While they'd successfully blacked out the Aspen Lodge, a full moon overhead cast light enough, reflected by snow on the ground, for Cody to spot a pair of shadow-shapes maneuvering to flank him, catch him in a crossfire, and eliminate him as a threat before they passed on to engage the Secret Service guards confined with their two charges in the lodge.

Cody imagined half a dozen methods they could use to clear the basement bunker, either capturing or killing those inside.

But first, they had to get past Jack.

He focused on the nearer of his enemies, assuming only two had been assigned to hit the lodge, since any others would have joined in shooting at him. His SR-16 carbine had an Aimpoint T1 Micro Quadrant Sight attached via a Picatinny tail on top of its receiver, and it marked a chosen target with a red dot visible to marksmen without any telltale projection to alert a shooter's chosen prey.

Simply locate the dot on center mass and squeeze.

Jack had the carbine set for semiauto fire. One trigger stroke dispatched a single 5.56mm FMJ boat-tail projectile down range, traveling 1,037 yards per second toward impact.

His adversary didn't scream or thrash around as dying warriors often did in Hollywood productions. With a muffled grunt, he simply toppled over backwards and collapsed.

One down, and that left one to go.

***

Laurel Lodge

"If sitting here is meant to reassure us that we're safe," Shayna Harwood informed her guards, "it isn't working."

Marianna wished Shayna would just shut up and do what was expected of her—nothing, as per usual—but long experience had taught her that attempts to reason with her younger sibling were a waste of time. She'd seen her parents do that futile song and dance thousands of times—shouting, cajoling, ultimately caving in and letting Baby Shayna have her way.

Sometimes, like now, she thought what Shayna needed was a good old-fashioned spanking, and to hell with protestations that she was a grown-up woman now, entitled to pursue life as she chose to.

Not that either of their parents ever raised a hand to any of their children. Live-in nannies and expensive prep schools were expected to instill a concept of responsibility, self-discipline, and all that happy crappy while their father climbed the ladder of political success, supported by his wife, enhanced by her exotic beauty and inherent charm.

And now, in Marianna's view, it was too late for Shayna to receive a personality transplant and finally, at twenty-five, begin to act her age.

In fact, it just might be too late for any of them, period.

"I'm serious," Shayna was fuming. "When can we get out of here?"

Rupert Malcolm was huddled with his fellow Secret Service agents, or at least the four of them who'd followed him into the basement bunker. Two more prowled around the lodge upstairs, lights out, the aggravating house alarm and flashing amber beacons all disabled now.

So far, there'd been no sound denoting contact with their enemies, whoever and however many of them there might be.

The first day of their long weekend at Camp David had turned into a nightmare, and all indications pointed toward it getting worse. Above all else, the fact that this might be her End of Days made Marianna furious. Still in her mid-twenties, as healthy as the proverbial horse, she'd nonetheless begun to think that she might never make it into open air again.

At least, not while she was alive.

Shayna's voice raked across her eardrums now, like nails on a chalkboard.

"Rupert! I asked you how much longer we'll be stuck down here, and I expect an answer!"

Something snapped in Marianna's mind. Turning to face her sister at the far end of a couch they shared, she spoke before Agent Malcom could try placating Shayna for the umpteenth time.

"Goddamn it, Shayna, will you just for once shut up?"

Her sister blinked at Marianna then, as if her words had been a slap across that pouty face.

"I beg your pardon. All I want is—"

Marianna shouting now. "Shut up! Shut up right now! We're all in this together, come what may. There's not a person in the world who wants to hear you bitch and moan, Shayna. We've all been there, done that, and I can promise you that everyone is sick to death of it. If you can't keep the whining to yourself, for God's sake find a closet, get inside, and lock the door behind you!"

Shayna gaped at her, wide-eyed, lips moving silently. In that moment, she looked to Marianna like a fish stranded ashore, drowning in open air.

And then, as if on cue, Shayna burst into tears.

Disgusted with her sister, with herself, and with the whole damned situation, Marianna rose and crossed the buried strong room, opening its minifridge. Inside, canned soft drinks vied for space with liquor bottles of the size dispensed by flight attendants to their airline's customers.

"Stoli, Jim Beam, Jose Cuervo," said Marianna, reeling off the brand names. "Anybody care to join me?"

Turning back to face the Secret Service agents and her sister, all regarding her as if she'd grown a second head within the past few seconds, Marianna found no takers.

"Okay, then," she told the others. "More for me."

At the same time, she imagined Cody moving through the dark woods, somewhere overhead.

And thought, *Jack, where in hell are you?*

***

Rosebud Cabin

Tina Harwood had finally succumbed to sleep, blessedly terminating her incessant questions about why she and her parents had been relegated to a basement, covered by armed men. Watching her doze now, her father Gary felt a pang of jealousy, wishing he shared his daughter's innocence and ignorance about the cold, cruel world.

Greta was holding Tina on her lap, rocking her slowly in an overstuffed wing chair and murmuring the last strains of a lullaby that had already done its job. Gary stood on the far side of their claustrophobic hideaway, hoping their Secret Service guards would come up with a lie to put his mind at ease.

But so far, damn it, they had only spoken the unappetizing truth.

Camp David under siege, and how long would it be before assistance reached them from the outside world?

Nobody seemed to have a clue.

Until this evening, Gary believed his life had been on track, proceeding as he'd hoped it would from childhood, when he first became fixated on the goal of a career in engineering. Most boys passed through stages, first imagining themselves in some adventurous profession—law enforcement firefighting, the military, maybe even toiling as a cowboy born a century too late—but Gary was the rare exception, focused on a single academic goal that made his male friends roll their eyes, while girls stared blankly at him, vaguely dazed by talk of optimization, applied probability, and stochastic modeling.

Despite all that, Gary had persevered, attending the Georgia Institute of Technology because it ranked first among ten universities offering IE degrees, earning a B.A. and M.S. in turn, stopping short of a doctorate because so many firms came calling with offers of lucrative employment.

And the rest, as somebody once said, was history.

Now, looking back from his present predicament, Gary wondered if he shouldn't have tried...something a little different.

Not giving up his dream career, mind you, but maybe taking time out for a tour of duty with the U.S. military, learning weapons inside-out, along with hand-to-hand combat techniques. Too much? At least he could have studied martial arts in his spare time away from class and work, maybe explaining it to Greta (and himself) as an extension of the P.E. classes that were mandatory during high school, an amusing way to keep himself in shape.

But it was too late now.

Men he'd never met or even heard of, spurred by motives yet unknown, were threatening his life and those he held most dear, and Gary Harwood didn't have a clue regarding how he should react beyond blindly accepting orders from his Secret Service guardians.

It was surreal to know he even *had* a federal security detail assigned to shadow him around the clock, in case some crazy with a grudge against his father or the government in general tried to express his anger through raw violence.

Still, Gary couldn't blame his father. He believed that Martin Harwood was a cut above most modern U.S. presidents, and any stride toward progress would face angry opposition in a nation of 328 million citizens, 89 percent of them armed with at least one firearm at last count.

But if he couldn't blame his father, couldn't blame the

country that he loved, and dared not blame himself, who did that leave?

No one. And that was driving Gary Harwood up the freaking feroconcrete wall.

Dejected, Gary asked Agent Pat Murphy, "Is there anything at all that I can do?"

"Afraid not, sir," Murphy replied. "Until we hear back from Agent Schumacher, all that anyone of us can do is sit and wait."

✳✳✳

Aspen Lodge

Adriaan Coetzee was shitting bricks.

Not literally true, but he was seething with a combination of anxiety and rage that his nerves on edge, reflected by a minor trembling of his hands.

Hans Behrens was—make that *had been*—Coetzee's best friend since he'd been cashiered from the SFB Recces for executing six Séléka rebels in the Central African Republic seven years ago. There'd been no formal court-martial, since the last thing Pretoria desired was more adverse publicity, but Coetzee had been shit-canned all the same and left to make a living from the private sector, peddling the only skills that he possessed.

Tonight was meant to be his last job as a mercenary. The pay on offer for this *verdoem* high-risk mission was enough to last him for the next five years, as long as he was relatively frugal and came out of it alive.

But now, his last friend in the world was dead and the *dom-kop* who had killed him had the same in mind for Coetzee, damn his eyes.

Now, all he had to do was find the *bliksem* and eliminate him.

Coetzee was ready with his Colt CQBR, its M203 launcher loaded with an M576 40mm buckshot cannister containing twenty metal pellets. And if all else failed, he had a 9×19mm Parabellum Vektor SP1 produced by South Africa's Denel Land Systems, and should the fight go hand-to-hand, he wore a Bauchop custom fighting knife.

But if he had a choice, Coetzee would rather drop his adversary with a killing rifle shot, then move on toward completion of his mission, taking out the U.S. president.

Edging around the spot where Behrens fell to rise no more, Coetzee thought he heard something on his left flank. Had it been a footstep crunching into snow?

He spun in that direction, leveling his Mark 18, but then a sharp blow like the stroke of a pickaxe pierced Coetzee's chest and he was falling, helpless to control his limbs as they convulsed. He landed on his back, eyes staring at the full moon overhead until a man's shadow blotted it out.

The man who'd killed him stared at Coetzee for a moment, then pronounced the last words he would ever hear.

"You lose, asshole."

CHAPTER 10

Approaching Wye Oaks Fitness Center

Nick Blair never cared for feeling foolish. He was a professional who knew weapons and tactics, but when working for one of the world's top arms dealers, he had deemed it wise to offer no objection when Thad Resnikoff offered to outfit his mercenaries with a relatively new piece of technology at no charge, to facilitate their multimillion-dollar mission.

Sadly, when you took a freebie, sometimes you wound up getting exactly what you'd paid for—which was squat.

There was nothing wrong with the item per se. Raytheon's Warrior-X wearable shooter detection system for soldiers weighed only twelve ounces and rode one shoulder of a war fighter's tactical vest, providing wearers with immediate hostile sniper fire and, when coordinated among members of a squad like Blair's, provided grid coordinates to facilitate elimination of hostiles out to a distance of three thousand yards. As a soldier moved in response to some threat, the Boomerang Warrior-X compensated for the wearer's motion and continually updated the enemy's location on a wrist display.

Brilliant, no doubt about it. Blair knew that on desert battlegrounds throughout Iraq, Afghanistan, and similar wide-open spaces, the device had been a literal life-saver time and time again. It ruled flat country when the chips were down.

But in a forest, not so much.

Blair had suspected that Camp David's wooded acreage would render the device useless, and he'd been right. He took no pleasure from that knowledge, but at least his patron wouldn't be deducting any portion of Blair's earnings from the raid as compensation for a flawed idea. And, thankfully, the Boomerang weighed just about the same as one loaded box magazine for an assault rifle.

Blair put it out of mind, therefore, as he approached Camp David's sprawling Wye Oak fitness center, trailed by Nino Nazzari and Marcel Bouchez. They weren't expecting to find any active targets at the fitness center, but Blair had to check it out, bearing in mind that members of the presidential party—or its Secret Service detail killing downtime—might have slipped away to have a workout before turning in, after a day of hassling over problems in the Middle East with more on tap tomorrow.

Blair had not expected to find anyone around the fitness center, but the layout was too large for him to pass it by without a check-in to confirm his hunch. The flip side of his expectation was a possibility that refugees from nearby cabins—Spruce, White Pine and Cypress—or surviving stragglers from the USMC barracks might have gravitated toward the gym, hoping to hide out there while they regrouped, and maybe find more friendlies gathering.

As it happened, though, Blair's first assumption proved correct. He swept Wye Oak's perimeter with Bouchez and Nazzari, satisfied himself that no one was concealed there, and instructed his subordinates to take it down.

"C-4," he said. "You know the drill. Two-minute fuses, then we're out of here."

Both mercenaries nodded to him in the darkness, offered Blair no verbal affirmation as they split up, double-timing off in separate directions to begin planting their plastique charges.

If he'd overlooked someone hiding inside the fitness center, Blair wasn't concerned about it. They would either die in the coming explosions or when tons of rubble buried them. More to the point, he would eradicate Wye Oak as a potential rally point for others that his team missed on their first sweep of the property.

Camp David might have been in use since FDR was president, but if Blair had his way tonight, the whole damned thing was coming down.

✳✳✳

Approaching Holly Cabin

If Secret Service agents ran a betting pool on which assignments were most dangerous, most would have put their money down on presidential visits overseas, particularly to the Middle East or sub-Saharan Africa. If asked to name the duty that was *least* likely to get him killed, Agent Jeff Schumacher would have selected guarding dignitaries at Camp David.

In Schumacher's opinion, the retreat was more secure than any site in Washington, including the White House and U.S. Capitol. Any demented loser who was halfway literate—

or had a functioning TV set—could eventually find his way to what J. Edgar Hoover used to call the "Seat of Government". And once they made it to D.C., the crazy bastards only had to watch and wait.

Camp David, by contrast, while often mentioned in the media, was tucked away and out of sight amidst Catoctin Mountain Park's six thousand-plus acres of rolling hills and forest, deleted from official maps, beneath a monitored umbrella of restricted air space.

In effect, the presidential getaway was hiding in plain sight.

So, sure, Schumacher would have called the compound safe, within the limits of that term as it applied to planet Earth in the third decade of a violent, chaotic century.

And he'd have lost that bet tonight, hands down.

So far, Schumacher hadn't glimpsed a hostile since he'd drawn the scouting mission from Laurel Lodge. He'd checked two of the nearest cabins, Sycamore and Linden, confirming they were both unoccupied before he moved toward Holly and Hawthorn. It struck him as a risky waste of time, but he was under orders, duty-bound to do as he was told.

Schumacher's only weapon was his standard-issue SIG Sauer P226 loaded with fifteen .357 rounds, plus two spare mags of fourteen cartridges apiece in pouches on his left hip. In the present circumstances, he would have preferred a carbine or an SMG, but Agent Malcolm—his immediate superior—wanted the heavy firepower to stay at Laurel Lodge, guarding the Harwood sisters.

What a pair they were, both lookers, but aside from that as different as night and day. Shayna was spoiled and seemed to be proud of it, wielding her sense of entitlement as if it were a writ from the Supreme Court granting her authority to flout whatever rules got in her way of having a good time.

Her older sister, on the other hand—while affable enough—was more reserved, making Schumacher think that she was still trying to figure out her place in life, eschewing Shayna's tendency to leave a string of problems in her wake for others to resolve.

Schumacher's next stop, Holly Cabin, meant a check-in with the Mossad agents covering Prime Minister Jairus Abramson, the first family's guest of honor this visit and—at least in Schumacher's opinion—the probable primary target for murder this morning.

President Harwood had his share of enemies, like any other politician who had occupied the White House, but Israel's prime minister took danger to another level altogether. Loathed by Muslims the world over, not to mention crackpot "alt-right" fascists and the full-bore lunatics who followed them online, Abramson literally couldn't step outside without a Kevlar vest and bodyguards up the wazoo.

Schumacher hoped the agents guarding Abramson at Holly Cabin wouldn't take him for a terrorist and gun him down before he had a chance to speak, but just in case, Jeff meant to take his time, go slow, and try his best to stay alive.

He almost made it. Holly Cabin coming into sight, when movement in the trees to his left-front warned Schumacher of danger lurking there. He swung the SIG in that direction, index finger shifting from its place outside the pistol's trigger guard to curl around the double-action trigger. It would only take a ten-pound pull to send a shot down range once he'd acquired a target.

But he never got the chance.

Schumacher heard a muffled *chug* and staggered backward as the bullet drilled his sternum, dead-on for the heart. He was already gone before his body toppled forward, landing face-down in the snow.

Approaching Rosebud Cabin

"Who all are we expecting here?" Owen McConnell asked.

"It should be Gary Harwood's family and their security detail," Sara Durell replied.

They had been keeping conversation to a minimum while trekking through the woods by moonlight, frozen snow crunching under their shoes. That noise was unavoidable, for either friend or foe, and they had paused repeatedly during their hike north from the helipad, to listen for the sound of infiltrators on the move.

So far, nothing.

"They'll have the standard Secret Service team, I guess?" McConnell said, in a near-whisper.

"Should be," Sara granted. "Female agents for the wife and daughter would be mandatory."

"And they're bound to be on edge." McConnell's tone told Sara that he was concerned about a hair-trigger reaction from the feds, shoot now and skip the questions America's first son, his wife and only child were under threat of kidnapping or death.

Sara tried her cell phone again and got the same result—or lack thereof—as on her previous attempts. If nothing else, she had to give the strike team credit for their choice of jamming gear.

They were a hundred yards or so southwest of Rosebud Cabin now and closing in, slowing their pace as they drew nearer. Standard practice told her that the Secret Service team assigned to Gary Harwood's family should have them stashed below ground now, although at least a pair of agents would remain on the cabin's ground floor—or possibly outside, near-by—to head off any infiltrators who approached.

"If they've got SR-25s, I hope they recognize us," said Mc-Connell.

"Maybe we should break out a white flag," Sara replied.

The semiautomatic KAC SR-25 was standard issue for the Secret Service Countersniper Support Unit, chambered for

7.62×51mm NATO cartridges, fed from ten- or twenty-round box magazines. Its standard Leupold Mark 4 Mil-dot riflescope enabled shooters to measure the range to objects of known size, the size of objects at known distances, compensating both for bullet drop and wind drift at known ranges, punching consistent half-inch groups out to one hundred yards.

In other words, the very distance Blades and Sara stood from Rosebud Cabin now.

Another step or two should tell the tale, whether they lived or died.

***

Outside Aspen Lodge

Two hostiles down, and Cody had no clue as to how many more remained at large.

He had a choice to make: duck back inside the lodge, get word to Agent Wilkins that he'd dealt with two of the compound's invaders, or move on in search of others. As it stood right now, Cody decided that retracing steps could be a costly waste of time.

However many adversaries might be prowling through Camp David, he knew damned well that there must be more than two. The threat persisted, even though he'd shaved the odds a bit. Finding and taking down the rest was Cody's top priority, and no one from the president's security detail could help him get it done.

His next target, barring an ambush by the infiltrators, would be Rosebud Cabin. Gary Harwood, with his wife and daughter, were sequestered there and under guard. If Jack could reunite them with the president and his first lady, it should strengthen the resolve of all concerned—and, incidentally, double the force of Secret Service agents watching over them.

And after that...

"Slow down," Cody muttered to himself. "Just take it one step at a time."

And try like hell to stay alive until sunrise.

He guessed at what was happening outside Camp David now. Communication between the retreat and Secret Service headquarters in Washington, was mandatory. Cody didn't know the schedule offhand, but he was certain that by now, considering the time elapsed from hostile penetration of the presidential getaway, alarm bells must be chiming at 950 H Street Northwest. Failing to reach the camp by telephone, by radio or Skype, Director James Murray and Deputy Director William Callahan would be on red alert by now and scrambling an Emergency Response Team, likely from the Baltimore field office at 100 South Charles Street.

Whether that relief could reach the camp without a major firefight was an open question. Cody's job, although he hadn't been assigned to it per se, was dealing with as many hostiles as he could, enabling the cavalry to save the day.

Whatever that required, he was prepared to see it through. If he survived to see the smoke clear, that would be a bonus.

If he didn't…well, at least the wags at Langley could say that he'd justified the nickname cowards only dared to use when he was out of earshot: "Suicide".

***

Rosebud Cabin

British mercenaries Ben Laughlin and Tony Graham stood beneath a looming oak, its shadow shielding them from lookouts stationed at their target destination's windows. Both, like all the other members of Blair's team, were dressed in snow camouflage from helmet covers down to cargo pants, with steel-toed insulated combat boots. Their hands and faces, likewise, had been streaked with gray and white combat cosmetics.

Although veterans of rival services—the SAS and SBS—Loughlin and Graham both had fought for queen and country in Afghanistan, Iraq and Syria. Graham had also done a tour in Libya, fresh out of Sterling Lines at Hereford, when the SAS pitched in to aid rebels in toppling Muammar Gaddafi's rogue regime. He'd missed out on the warlord's execution by Misrata militiamen but had arrived in time to see Gaddafi with a broken broom handle protruding from between his buttocks.

Wild times in the desert, all around.

"How many do you figure are inside?" Laughlin inquired.

"No telling," Graham answered. "But the boss wants all of

them."

"Too bad he couldn't spare the time to help out, eh?"

"RHIP, old son."

"Too right," Laughlin agreed.

Rank has its privileges, the time-honored enlisted man's lament.

Graham and Laughlin had no grudge against the strangers they had killed so far tonight, or those who still awaited death. It was a paying job that would allow them to retire, assuming that they both survived and seriously sought to end their stint as triggermen for hire.

One million U.S. dollars each, tax-free, paid into various numbered accounts scattered around the globe, from Vanuatu and Samoa to the Caymans, Seychelles, St. Lucia, or those old standbys: Switzerland, Monaco and Lichtenstein.

"We'd best get on with it," said Graham.

"Right you are."

Both mercs were armed with weapons they had used extensively while fighting for the Union Jack, MP5 submachine guns and Glock 17MB pistols, each seventeen 9mm Parabellum rounds packed in their staggered-column magazines, one in the chamber, and an ambidextrous magazine catch. Aside from firearms, they were well armed with grenades and C-4 charges, all topped off with Fairbairn–Sykes fighting knives carried by British troops around the world since 1941.

Something for everyone, no matter what it took to put a target down and out.

"No prisoners," Graham reminded his companion.

"And no witnesses."

"A clean sweep all the way."

"We're making history tonight, old son," Laughlin observed.

"The kind they never teach in school or talk about on tele."

"Who'd believe it, anyway?"

Graham was not precisely sure who they would find inside the Rosebud Cabin, and he didn't care. There'd been a time, when he was still a greenhorn, not yet blooded, when he might have said he'd joined the army to defend his homeland or to fight for those oppressed. Today, he didn't buy that codswallop or know many who did. A soldier fought for glory, sometimes for advancement, and above all else for pay.

Man-killing was a trade like any other. Those who practiced it extensively, efficiently, demanded higher rates than that raw recruits, regardless of their zeal.

After tonight, Graham supposed survivors of the Camp David attack could write their own tickets on any continent, with any paymaster.

And if he fell in battle, well, Graham had no one left to mourn his passing anyway.

✳✳✳

Rosebud Cabin

Gary Harwood sipped a glass of Dewars twelve-year-old Scotch—dubbed "The Ancestor"—and offered silent thanks to whichever emergency consultant had suggested stocking liquor in the Rosewood Cabin's bunker.

That was pre-need planning he could truly get behind.

Greta had spurned his offer of a drink, getting that little irritated wrinkle in between her perfect eyebrows. Tina was still sleeping, lucky girl, and Gary had known better than to tempt their Secret Service agents with a shot to calm their nerves. The smallest sip could get them fired, besides which Gary needed them to be in tip-top shape, whatever happened next, to keep him and his family alive.

He'd spent the last hour and change remembering attacks on other modern presidents.

Dallas was ancient history, but Gerald Ford had managed to survive two botched attempts by pistol-toting women in September of 1975. The lunatic who tried for Jimmy Carter four years later only brought a starter pistol and a box of blanks, which ultimately spared him doing time. Another nut, John Hinckley Jr., had left Ronald Reagan "close to death" in 1981 and spent the next thirty-five years in mental hospitals.

From there on to the present, no would-be assassins wounded anyone, though plenty more had tried: fourteen Iraqi agents hoped to kill Bush 41, four months after he left office, during a pointless visit to Kuwait. At least five bids to take Bill Clinton out had been reported in the media, three more botched plots against Bush 43, four racist runs against Barack Obama, and at least tries with Donald Trump. With the exception of al-Qaeda back on 9/11, none of the half-baked conspirators had posed a major threat.

But now...

There'd never been another plot like this one, even when a handful of Confederate fanatics managed to kill Lincoln and came close to gutting William Seward, missing Andrew Johnson altogether at the tag end of the Civil War.

Whoever was behind the raid against Camp David, for whatever reason, Gary understood there was a chance that they might pull it off, despite all the security in place—marines, the Secret Service, and a no-fly zone enforced by fully-loaded F-15 Eagles.

In fact, without any communication between buildings at the compound, Gary couldn't swear that either of his parents had survived this long. For all he knew, the plotters could have leveled Aspen Lodge and slaughtered everyone inside.

And here he sat, Waterford crystal whisky glass in hand, wishing that he was anywhere on Earth but at Camp David.

What did that say about Gary as a son, a husband, as a man?

He quaffed the dregs of scotch, then stiffened as a sound of crackling reached his ears. Whatever else the bunker might be—bombproof, its air filtered to prevent a chemical attack—sound from the world outside still managed to come through.

Gunfire.

The Secret Service agents trapped below ground moved in unison to guard the basement stairs, assault weapons shouldered and aiming at the fireproof access door. Gary rose from his chair and stood a few paces behind them, feeling ineffectual in his unarmed attempt to back up the professionals.

He knew Greta was watching him but dared not meet her
eyes.

For all the good it did, he offered up a silent prayer.

Let Tina sleep through whatever comes next.

Sara Durell and Blades McConnell came in from behind the
gunmen crouched in front of Rosebud Cabin, just in time to
see them drop a Secret Service agent on the porch with inter-
locking streams of submachine-gun fire.

By moonlight, Sara thought their victim looked Hispanic,
reasonably young, with close-cropped hair, but none of that
meant anything. Whoever he had been, the agent died defending people who had never been elected to a public office
in their lives, under the gun because of their familial relationship to President Harwood.

A second agent came out of the shadows to her left, around
the cabin's northwest corner, moving in a crouch, a shotgun
in his hands. He had a twelve-gauge buckshot round already
chambered, fired it from the hip, not taking time to aim, and
seemed to miss both targets on his first attempt.

The hostile shooters—terrorists? contract assassins?—answered him with automatic fire, cutting the agent's legs from
under him. He dropped but hung onto his Remington, jacking
another round into the shotgun's chamber even as he fell.

The guy had guts, and then some, but raw courage wouldn't
compensate for blood loss from ruptured femoral arteries.
A wound like that—*two* wounds, in fact, twin jets of blood

steaming on contact with the frosty air—would kill a man in five, six minutes tops, unless he made it into triage right away.

And while there was supposed to be a navy doctor somewhere on the grounds, always assigned to presidential parties—he or she was nowhere to be found just now.

Screw this, she thought, and fired a short burst from her borrowed SR-16 carbine, watched one of the cabin's camouflaged attackers lurch and drop. She had no qualms about back-shooting him, had never understood that macho bullshit from the Western films her father used to watch on weekends, cheering on John Wayne or Randolph Scott.

If enemies were dumb enough to turn their backs on her, to hell with them.

McConnell fired the pistol she had given him, and Sara saw the other infiltrator lurch, stagger and fall while he was turning to confront them. She was pleased about the easy kills, when suddenly, down range, both adversaries cut loose with their SMGs, a storm of bullets rippling overhead, slicing through branches long devoid of leaves.

"Kevlar?" McConnell asked, as he dropped to a prone firing position at her side.

"Or something like it," Sara answered back. "Looks like they're wearing helmets, too."

Ballistic helmets, vests, and other gear were readily available from countless sources, ranging from the Internet to bigbox stores around the world. The only limitation on access was money, and she knew that someone who could mount a full-scale raid against Camp David must have ample cash to spread around.

"Go for the face or neck if possible," she told McConnell, guessing he'd already had the same thought without voicing it.

"Small targets," he replied, but fired another round off from his SIG P229 from forty feet or so. That time, one of the camo-clad shooters cried out and slapped a hand against his throat, on the left side.

The wounded gunman's partner sprayed another burst of submachine-gun fire in her direction, spoiling Sara's shot but missing her a second time.

With any luck, that just might be his last mistake.

***

Tony Graham watched a pool of blood spreading beneath Ben Laughlin's inert form. It looked jet-black by winter moonlight, steam rising as winter chilled the small lake's starting 98.6 degrees.

Before much longer, Graham knew, the blood would start to freeze, resembling an oil slick where it had congealed with snow.

One second, Laughlin had been fighting back against their enemies, and then…

To hell with it.

Graham couldn't begin to count the men whose deaths he'd witnessed, many of them caused by his own hand. Laughlin had been a pal of sorts, but war had schooled him in the risks of friendship, there one minute, blown away the next.

It would have done no good for him to mourn Laughlin, even if Graham were still capable of such emotion. And, if he were honest with himself, he simply didn't have that in him anymore.

What moved him now was a compulsion to fight back and to survive the night.

He was outnumbered, but an edge of two-to-one was not what he'd have called a great advantage for his enemies. The worst odds he had ever faced alone—nineteen on one—had failed to take him out, and Graham saw no reason to believe a paltry pair of adversaries would succeed while so many had failed before them.

All he had to do was keep his wits about him, use the skills he had acquired in military training, finely honed by battle, and there was no reason why he couldn't stick around to claim his million dollars when the smoke cleared.

Killing was his job, and up to now, he'd always done it well enough.

Suspecting that his MP5 was running low on Parabellum ammo, Graham yanked its magazine and fed a fresh one into the receiver, cranking back the non-reciprocating cocking handle located above the SMG's handguard on its left side. Peering into the dappled moonlight forty-some-odd feet in front of him, he scanned for any shapes or movement that would let him single out a target.

So far, nothing.

Why had they stopped firing? Even after putting Laughlin

down, his opposition had to know—or guess, at least—that Graham was alive.

Or if they didn't...

That could be the very edge he needed. Wait until one of them couldn't take it anymore and started forward to investigate. With any luck, both enemies might make the move together, giving him a chance to cut them down.

But if they stalled too long, or tried outflanking him...

Graham moved cautiously away from Laughlin's corpse, relieved when no one spotted him and opened fire. The Rosebud Cabin's porch had half a dozen upright posts supporting its shake-shingled roof, and Graham wedged himself behind one of them, shielded for the moment from incoming fire.

That done, he unclipped a fragmentation grenade from his tactical vest, weighing the lethal egg in his left hand, taking his time to pluck its safety pin. A pitch from where he lay would not be easy, but he reckoned he could manage it, a sidearm throw with everything he had behind it, pitching for effect without expecting pinpoint accuracy.

The M68 frag grenade has an M217 electrical impact fuse, primed to blow within two seconds of touchdown, plus a backup pyrotechnic delay function that initiates detonation three to seven seconds after the impact fuse fails. Either way, human targets would have to be spry if they hoped to avoid its spray of metal fragments with a sixteen-foot kill radius, wounding expected at three times that range.

If nothing else, the blast should flush his enemies from cover, hopefully into his line of automatic fire.

He wound up, made the pitch, and raised his MP5 into alignment as he started counting down.

Jack Cody homed in on the sharp, staccato sound of gunfire in the night.

He was two hundred yards northwest of Rosewood Cabin, homing in, and worried that he might already be too late. The first son and his family were under guard there—or had been, at least—until the latest round of firing echoed through Camp David's wooded acreage.

And now?

The only way Cody could answer that was by proceeding to the site and seeing for himself.

When he was fifty-odd yards out and closing, an explosion echoed through the woodland. Cody saw the flash of a grenade blast, heard its shrapnel cutting into tree trunks, and jogged forward with his shoulders hunched instinctively. He went in fast and coming from behind the cabin, ready with his SR-16 Secret Service carbine as the porch came into view.

Off to his right, had saw two figures reeling from the frag grenade's explosion, firing short bursts toward the cabin's porch where one man lay unmoving and a second—in the same winter camouflage garb—was milking short bursts from a submachine gun toward the blast survivors at the tree line.

Cody didn't have to guess which side he should support. After the flash, he couldn't make out any features of the warriors in the woods, but he knew damned well that Camp

David's guards were not decked out in snow-mountain camo fatigues.

That made the dead guy and his lively sidekick enemies.

Jack didn't hesitate from that point on, snapping the carbine to his shoulder, squeezing off a three-round burst that struck the sole surviving infiltrator underneath his raised right arm and staggered him. Cody could hear him grunt as impact knocked the wind out of his lungs, but even with a hit to center mass, the camo man recovered swiftly, pivoting to fire his next burst Cody's way.

Jack didn't hesitate, just switched his SR-16 to full auto and unloaded half a magazine into the patch of darkness just above the submachine gun's winking muzzle. Half a dozen 5.56mm boat-tail slugs punched through the gap between his camouflaged helmet and SMG. There should have been a face there, and perhaps there was—but not for long.

"You two all right?" Cody called out to the members of his home team who'd been under fire.

A voice he recognized responded, with another question. "Cody? Is that you?"

"Sara," he said. "Glad I could make if for the third act."

"So am I," she answered, moving toward him through the moonlight, with Owen McConnell on her heels. "A minute longer and you might have missed it."

"Better late than never, I suppose," he said. "Now, how about we have a look inside?"

CHAPTER 11

Laurel Lodge

Marianna Harwood checked her watch, nearly despairing when she noted how much time had passed since the attack began.

The lodge's backup generator had shut down an hour and fifteen minutes earlier, casting their bunker refuge into darkness until Secret Service flashlights let their guards retrieve six Coleman battery-powered twin LED lanterns to repel the brooding dark.

One of the Secret Service agents, making small talk meant to soothe the Harwood sisters—and perhaps himself, as well—informed Shayna and Marianna that each lantern had adjustable brightness ranging from high to "ultra-low". On "high", one lamp provided 390 "extra-bright" lumens, lighting up a thirty-two-foot radius, the lowest setting furnished 100 "bright" lumens on the lowest setting, illuminating a nineteen-foot circle. Depending on the level chosen, eight D-cell batteries had a life expectancy ranging from eighty-five to two hundred ninety-nine hours.

Shayna has asked why it couldn't be three hundred hours exactly, but that stumped their guards, who'd responded with shrugs. At least, one of them said, the lanterns came with a five-year limited warranty.

Unable to resist, Shayna had answered back, "So, they go dark in less than thirteen days, but we have five years to return them? I am *so* relieved to know that Treasury can get its money back!"

At that point, Agent Malcom intervened, saying, "We know that help is on the way."

"Do we?" Shayna replied. "The phones and radios are jammed. We can't set foot upstairs, much less outside. How do you *know* what's going on out there, Rupert?"

"Miz Harwood—"

"It's a valid question," Marianna said.

All eyes were on her now, no one appearing more surprised than she was, at herself, for jumping in on Shayna's side.

Agent Malcom, for his part, just seemed disappointed in her. "Miz Harwood—"

"It's too confusing with the courtesy," she cut him off. "Can't we just use first names?"

Malcom winced that that idea, but said, "Yes, Marianna. As you wish. No one's suggesting that we'll be down here for two weeks, much less for five years."

"Of course not," Shayna piped up. "Since we'd all be *dead* by them. My question was, how do you know what's happening out there? You can't even reach out to ask the agents you left topside."

"There are certain protocols," the head of their security detail replied. "Check-ins by phone or radio with Secret Service headquarters and the Catoctin Naval Base. When those calls don't go through on schedule, it triggers a reaction."

"What time is the next contact supposed to happen?" Marianna asked him.

Malcom checked his watch by lamplight, frowned, and told her, "Ninety minutes, give or take."

"That's sounding loosey-goosey," Shayna chided him.

"My watch isn't precisely synchronized with headquarters on Washington or with the camp commander's office."

"So, we have to wait another hour and a half, *approximately*, before anybody knows that we're in trouble?" Shayna pressed.

"Unless some other circumstance alerts authorities outside of the perimeter," Malcom allowed.

"Like the explosions we've already heard," said Marianna.

"Like that, yes," Malcom agreed.

She followed up, asking, "In which case...what?"

"If someone heard the blasts and called the sheriff's office—"

"Where's that located," asked Marianna.

"Based in Frederick," said Malcom, but they have a substation in Emmitsburg."

"How far away is that?" Shayna inquired, tag-teaming him.

"Fourteen miles northwest of us, approximately," Malcom answered.

"And the deputies, whoever," Marianna followed through, would come to have a look?"

"Doubtful," said Malcom. "The protocol would be to contact federal authorities. Could be the Secret Service, FBI, the navy—maybe all of the above."

"So," Shayna chimed in, "either someone knows that we need help, or else they won't know for another ninety minutes, right?"

"That sums it my, Miz—"

Loud noises above ground suddenly distracted Agent Malcom, drawing his eyes to the bunker's feroconcrete ceiling.

"What was that?" asked Marianna, hating that she sounded frightened now.

"My guess," Malcom replied, "would be gunfire."

✳✳✳

"You think they make it easy on purpose?" Tom Altman asked.

"Don't ask me, yo," replied Fabius Worthy. "I just work here, same as you."

"But making better money than the Secret Service," Altman said.

"If I live long enough to spend it, man."

"You know what Blair would say, right?"

"Yeah. He'd say that's up to me."

"Okay, then. We've got two of 'em so far. My guess would be the rest are in the basement."

Worthy did his best impression of an elevator jockey in

some big department store. "Cosmetics, men's wear, ladies' lingerie."

"And hostages," Alton appended, with a crooked smile.

"We may as well get to it, then," Worthy allowed.

"It's your show," Alton replied. "You've got the big gun."

"That's what she said, yo," Worthy replied, and laughed at his own joke.

His gun was big, all right, meaning the PSG1 manufactured by Heckler & Koch of Oberndorf am Neckar, Germany. The "PSG" stood for *Präzisionsschützengewehr*, translated from German as "precision shooter rifle", and the weapon absolutely lived up to its mouthful of a name.

The *big* part was immediately obvious. It measured 48.4 inches overall, with a 25.6-inch barrel, and weighed in at just under sixteen pounds unloaded. A semiautomatic piece, the PSG1 fed 7.62×51mm NATO—adapted from the classic .300 Savage—from five-, ten- or twenty-round detachable box magazines. A fifty-round drum was also offered, but most snipers felt it added too much weight for practicality in combat. The weapon's effective range was one thousand meters—the best part of 3,300 feet—with pinpoint accuracy promised by its Hensoldt ZF 6×42 PSG1 telescopic sight with illuminated reticle. That sight's reticle is in the first image level, so it changes as a shooter zooms in or out, but the middle red dot is in the second image level, unaltered regardless of magnification.

In a word: perfection.

Worthy's targets at that moment were two men in black,

presumably both Secret Service, armed with automatic rifles in their gloved hands, sidearms hidden underneath their overcoats. Not that they'd have a chance to reach their pistols—or, for that matter, get much use out of their long guns.

Fabius Worthy might not be the brightest bulb in any given chandelier, but when it came to long-range accuracy with the rifle of his choice, he ranked among the mercenary world's elite.

Altman watched the ex-Navy SEAL lime up his first shot, keeping quiet to avoid distracting Worthy from the kill. Waiting for Hell to come calling on Earth, Altman was grateful for the SureFire EP4 Sonic Defender shooter's earplugs that he wore. They felt a little stuffy going in, but that beat going deaf, in Altman's reckoning.

He watched now from a yard behind Worth and offset to his partner's left. Fabius chose one of the two agents stationed outside of Laurel Lodge, centered him in the Hensoldt scope, and stroked the PSG1's trigger.

Down range, Altman saw the agent's head explode, reminding him of how a .44 Magnum might burst a watermelon. Blood and brains spattered the second guard, delaying his reaction for a crucial second while Worthy adjusted for his second shot and sent another 7.62mm slug hurtling toward lethal impact.

Splat!

Another skull dissolved, the body it had once directed through its daily movements going limp and dropping to the porch already slick with gore.

"Not bad," Altman allowed.

"Not bad? I'm freaking perfect, yo."

"And modest, too. Come on. Let's clean house and move on."

***

"Sounds like a sniper's rifle," Blades McConnell said.

Jack Cody couldn't argue that point with him. "Two rounds, rapid fire," he said. "The shooter's either jumpy, or he's damned good at his job."

"Whoever set this up," Sara Durell advised, "they're using pros."

Jack didn't want to sell the Secret Service short, especially since many of the agents who had joined since 9/11 had seen far-flung combat in the War on Terrorism, but he wasn't harboring illusions on that score, either. Private military companies these days were offering top dollar when it came to salaries for proven veterans and specialists, dwarfing the salaries available to special agents of the U.S. government, be they recruited by the ATF, the DEA, the FBI or Secret Service.

Starting salary for feds was $47,000 yearly, topping out at double that around retirement age. Meanwhile, most PMC payouts ranged from $500 to $750 per day—meaning $15,000 and $22,500 per month, or $180,000 to $270,000 per year. Idealistic warriors might draw satisfaction from government service—or even stay in the army, where a master sergeant with twenty years in uniform banked $50K yearly—but

Earth, as "Queen of Pop" Madonna Ciccone once sang—was a crassly material world.

Money talked, and talent generally walked in pursuit of top dollar.

Still, the first two mercs that Cody had encountered outside Alpine Lodge had tested their skill against his and come out on the losing end. Maybe that indicated hasty hiring on their sponsor's part, or it could be a nod to Cody's private attitude.

A soldier with nothing to live for has nothing to lose.

"So, remind me who's in Laurel Lodge," McConnell said.

Sara answered him, saying, "The Harwood sisters."

"Ouch," Blades muttered. "There's a pair to draw to."

"Marianna's not so bad, from what I hear," Sara replied. Turning to Cody then, she asked, "You know her, don't you, Jack?"

"We've met," Cody replied and left it there.

"A sound endorsement if I've ever heard one," said McConnell.

Feeling cornered, Cody elaborated. "She's no Shayna, if that helps."

"Better or worse?" Blades asked him in a teasing tone of voice.

"Let's say I haven't had to pull her out of any love nests with a hit team breathing down our necks, and let it go at that," Cody said.

" 'Nuff said," McConnell granted. "We're not here to judge a popularity contest."

"Just kicking ass and taking names," Sara chimed in.

So far, they'd only heard two shots from Laurel Lodge, but Cody thought about the C-4 charges detonated outside Alpine Lodge and reckoned they were wasting time on chatter.

"What say we get on with it," he said, "before these assholes huff and puff and blow the damned house down."

"We need to turn the lamps down," Agent Rupert Malcolm said.

Shayna Harwood couldn't resist another jab at him for that. "Because we'll all be so much safer in the dark."

"I want to turn them *down* Miz Harwood," Malcom answered back. "Not *off.*"

"My bad," Shayna replied. "So, what's the plan?"

"We should assume for now that we've lost Agents Fitzroy and Zvirblis."

"You think they're both dead?" Marianna asked.

"I hate to say it," Malcom told her, "but we only heard two rifle shots, and neither of them had a caliber to match those. Without confirmation that they're still alive and in the game, we can't afford to count on them."

"That's cold," Shayna advised.

"Miz Harwood, that's reality," Malcom replied.

"Uh-huh. You don't mind if I keep on hoping they're okay, though? Does that go against your protocol?"

"Hope never hurts," Malcom allowed. "As long as you're not banking on it."

Marianna cut through the small talk, asking, "Rupert, you think they're coming after us down here, don't you?"

"I can't see any other reason why they're going through all this," he said.

"And we should take for granted that they'll go after our parents too, right? After Gary's family as well?"

Shayna jumped in, adding, "And don't forget about the PM while you're at it."

Marianna nodded. Said, "With all of that in mind, suspecting we're two agents down already, don't you think we should have something we can use in self-defense? I mean, in case they breach the access doors?"

"Defending you is our job," Malcom said, sternly.

"And you're a pro, I get it," Marianna countered. "But your men upstairs were both pros, right? And if they didn't even get a shot off, well..."

"What are you asking me, Miz Harwood?"

"What I'm *saying* is, I'd like to have a gun."

Their chief protector blinked at her and said, "That *is* a violation of our protocol."

"I get it, Rupert. But I promise not to shoot you or your men by accident. You want me to. I'll even promise not to fire a shot until you've all run out of bullets. How'd that be?"

"I'm sorry," Malcom said. "That's unacceptable."

"So, I'll just have to wait till they break in, then hope there's time to take one off your corpse if it comes down to that?"

"Miz Harwood—"

"Jesus!" Shayna started talking over him. "We've both had

shooting lessons and I still remember mine. Our father made it mandatory, back in junior high. I haven't thought about it in forever, and I never thought I'd hear myself say this, but I agree with Marianna."

"And I'd count your votes," Malcom replied, "if we were having a debate. No guns for protectees. That's carved in stone, ladies."

"We're *protectees,* now," Shayna fairly jeered. "Hell, that makes everything okay, right?"

"It's not open for discussion," Agent Malcom said. "Now, if you'll kindly let us focus on our job…"

Before he could complete that sentence, an explosion rocked the lodge upstairs. Shayna imagined she could hear a portion of the ceiling or wall collapse after the blast but guessed that might have been an echo ringing in her ears.

She'd hated basic firearms training when she was a young teenager, but this seemed to be a perfect time for second thoughts. With Marianna, she had also suffered through two months of martial arts training, her parents' hedge against an odd society that often seemed to punish who had suffered sexual assaults while giving their attackers a free pass.

How many of those moves did she recall today? Would muscle memory come back somehow to help her when the chips were down?

Shayna locked eyes with Marianna, read her elder sister's fear, and for the second time within as many days, hoped that she hadn't reached the rude conclusion of her life.

"They must already be inside," Owen McConnell said.

"Looks like it," Cody agreed.

Two bodies lay in pools of blood, not far apart on Laurel Lodge's wide front porch. Neither dead man wore snow-mountain camouflage fatigues, no helmets, and no combat boots, which told Cody they were—*had been*—Secret Service agents put to work as outer guards.

Remembering the shots he'd heard, and the two agents' near decapitation, he took for granted that the first to fall had never seen death coming for him, while his partner hadn't found time to react and save himself.

Two up, two down. And with the fleeting interval between those rifle shots, they would be squaring off against a seasoned shooter with a weapon far surpassing anything the three of them were carrying in terms of range.

Which didn't mean the game was hopeless going in.

From the two men assigned to Alpine Lodge, and the same number sent to Rosebud Cabin, Cody figured they were likely up against a pair of mercenaries, one of them a designated marksman, with the other's specialty unknown. A second later, when a high-explosive blast ripped through the lodge, Cody had that nagging question answered for him.

One merc was a sniper, clearly. His companion was the demolition guy.

"You think they want to bring the lodge down?" Sara asked.

"Not while they're still inside it," Cody replied. "That's

suicide."

Did he imagine Sara's sidelong glance in his direction, maybe wondering if that had been a slip of Cody's tongue?

Before he could assess that, Blades McConnell said, "They're likely working on the bunker's access door."

"Another charge or two like that one ought to bring it down," Cody replied. The notion of a bombproof door—unless it was a giant vault, like Colorado's Cheyenne Mountain Complex, housing NORAD and USNORTHCOM headquarters—had very little real-world application with the various explosives readily available.

"And once they blow the door—" McConnell said.

"We'll be too late," Cody finished up for him.

"I don't like going in there blind," Sara told them.

"Nobody in his right mind would," Cody said.

"But we still have to do it, right?" she asked.

"No way around it I can see," Cody agreed.

"Sometimes I hate it when I'm right," she groused.

"We all do," said McConnell, seeming taken by surprise when Cody and Sara laughed.

"No, wait," Blades said. "I didn't mean—"

"Forget it, Owen," Sara said. "I'm not pissed off. And even I was, it likely won't last more than two, three minutes."

"That's the spirit," Cody said. Added, "Remember that song from the early Nineties?"

"Can you vague that up a little?" Sara asked him.

"One line is, like, 'I'm a loser baby, so why don't you kill me?'"

"Beck sang that," McConnell said. "The title's 'Loser'."

"There you go."

"Hey, I'm not throwing in the towel, Jack," Sara argued back.

"I'm glad to hear it," Cody said, putting on a smile. "Now, prove it."

After countless nights on bivouac with Delta Force, Tom Altman wasn't big on camping, but he thought that Laurel Lodge would be all right for going rustic while remaining in the lap of luxury.

Somebody's tax dollars at work, pampering VIPs—but not Tom's dollars, since he'd given up on paying taxes after being booted from the army on a Section Eight.

That was a put-up deal on his part, starting after he'd discovered how much former soldiers with his skill set were collecting from a drove of PMCs around the world. He'd interviewed with half a dozen outfits before joining Blair's, his choice decided by an extra zero added to what other groups were offering, and there had been no looking back.

Now, he was in the middle of his last job, one way or another, and however it wound up, at least no one could say he hadn't given it his best shot all the way.

"A little help here, yo," Fabius Worthy called to Altman.

"Right. One block of C-4 coming up."

Worthy was standing ready by the lodge's bunker access door. Smiling off-kilter, he replied, "Sorry I had to interrupt your mind-porn, man. You back on busty Asian beauties?"

"Planning for retirement," Altman said.

"Uh-huh. Let's get the job done first, yo. Punch the time clock when it's done."

Altman surveyed the so-called bombproof door in front of him: a three-inch slab of tempered steel with hinges on the backside, meant to keep an enemy from breaking through. One thing the builders of such cages normally forgot—as in this case—was the surrounding wall. Feroconcrete was strong, but not impenetrable.

At least, not to someone with the proper tools in hand.

Altman started by gouging claylike pieces from the C-4 charge he'd just unwrapped, shaping them as he fastened each in turn against the wall along the door's left side. When that was done, he linked the beige blobs with a length of detonating cord to set them off in series when they blew.

Most sheeple—Altman's nickname for civilians—didn't know that Composition C explosive came in three strengths: C-2, C-3 and C-4. There had been a C1 prior to World War II, but C2 had replaced it with an added kick. C-4 was now top of the line, consisting of 89.9 percent RDX explosive, 10 percent butyl rubber for malleability, and 0.2 percent dye to give it the innocent façade of butter cream frosting on a birthday cake.

C-4 is stable and impervious to most physical shocks. It won't explode from being dropped, set afire, zapped in a microwave oven, or even by point-blank gunshots. Detonation is achieved only by shockwave, from a blasting cap or fuse designed for that purpose. When detonation is initiated, generating an explosive velocity of 26,550 feet per second, the compound instantly disintegrates, releasing nitrogen, water and carbon oxides, plus a smidge of other gases.

No one with a brain wishes to be on the receiving end.

"All set, yo?" Worthy asked him, when Altman had the three innocent-looking lumps of plastique affixed to the wall, linked in series by a dangling ribbon of det cord, a manual trigger attached at the cord's free end.

Altman said, "We're good to go, man."

"Righteous. Let's duck outa here and get it done."

Both mercs retreated onto Laurel Lodge's porch, ignored the bodies sprawling there, and crouched in preparation for the coming blast.

"Ready?" Altman asked Worthy.

"I was born that way, yo."

Smiling now, Altman announced, "Fire in the hole!" and pressed the trigger to unleash a little taste of Hell on Earth.

✳✳✳

"Goddamn it, we're too late!"

The edge on Sara's voice was diamond-hard, belying the expression on her face. She had reacted to the blast as if it were a sucker punch delivered to her gut, or the announcement of a loved one's passing in a highway pileup.

"Not so fast," Cody advised. "Don't throw the towel in yet."

"I second that," Owen McConnell said. "It only means somebody's seeking access to the bunker."

"Right," Sarah snapped. "With Semtex or whatever."

"Let's wait and see the damage first," Cody said, "before we count the home team out."

With that, the trio double-timed toward Laurel Lodge, still sixty yards or so distant through looming trees and shrubbery that snagged on clothing as they ran. Despite his admonition not to panic, Cody's heart was in his throat, unbidden scenes of carnage flashing through his mind.

The world's worst slasher movie playing in his head.

He'd spoken truthfully, suggesting that the Harwood sisters and their bodyguards might be alive despite the blast—perhaps even unscathed. He knew that Laurel Lodge had been built in 1972, the year of Richard Nixon's reelection, while the Watergate scandal was still a minor blip on the *Washington Post*'s radar screen, before the resignations in disgrace of Vice President Agnew, then Nixon himself, the latter pardoned by successor Gerald Ford as Tricky Dick boarded Marine One for his getaway.

Even the shamed president's harshest critics gave him brownie points for easing the Cold War, negotiating in apparent good faith with the Russians and Chinese. Still, planners working overtime in Washington, in Moscow and Beijing all knew that damned near anything could happen on the world stage, damned near anytime.

One thing you had to grant government engineers: they built bomb shelters to last forever and a day, particularly when the occupants were meant to be federal honchos from D.C. Nobody knew when someone might go *Dr. Strangelove*, launching a surprise attack and setting off a chain reaction that would set the world on fire. Whatever happened, and whoever's fault it was, the government's top dogs on both sides of the Iron Curtain wanted to survive, even if they had nothing left to rule but foul irradiated ash.

Plastique was nothing, next to nuclear warheads, but a hurtling warhead from Siberia, China, or a submarine prowling the seven seas, but shaped charges could be placed *precisely*, cracking strongholds that a massive airburst and resultant gamma rays might leave unscathed.

And if Camp David's infiltrators cracked the Rosebud Cabin bunker, they could slaughter Marianna, Shayna, and their Secret Service detail with grenades and small arms fire.

In which case, Cody and his two companions had no recourse but to execute the murderers on sight, move on from there to purge the presidential compound while they exorcised their rage.

"I see it!" Sara told her two companions, when they'd closed the gap to thirty yards or so.

"It doesn't seem to be on fire," McConnell said.

Small favors, Cody thought, then spotted movement on the lodge's porch, two men dressed in snow-mountain camouflage fatigues he'd seen before.

"They aren't in yet," he told Sara and Blades.

"You hope not, anyway," Sara replied.

"Whatever," said McConnell. "We've got two shooters outside. Let's move!"

A heartbeat later they were running, three abreast, to lift

the siege of Laurel Lodge.

✳✳✳

Fabius Worthy turned toward Tom Altman, meaning to tell him they should hustle up and get the wet work done, when Altman broke into a jerky little dance, dropping his Mark 18 CQBR, then staggering across the porch of Laurel Lodge.

Before Worthy could ask the white boy what in hell he reckoned he was doing, blood spouted from vents in Altman's snow-mountain fatigues and spattered Worth's face, feeling like warm oil on his skin, but with the smell of bright new pennies. By the time Altman collapsed across the toes of Worthy's combat boots, Fabius heard the sounds of automatic gunfire coming from the nearby tree line and he lunged headlong through the front door of Laurel Lodge, pursued by whining bullets but unscathed.

Fabius guessed that near miss had exhausted his good luck for this mission, and maybe for a month of Sundays afterward. On second thought, huddled against the building's stout log wall, he wondered if his luck wasn't tapped out for good.

As Worthy sometimes did at times of stress, he muttered to himself, saying, "I'm caught between a damned rock and a freaking hard place, yo."

Two or three shooters in the woods outside, and now he saw that Altman's C-4 charges had indeed shattered the basement access door's hinges, propelling it inside and down a flight of concrete stairs into a chamber where a warm glow emanated, putting Fabius in mind of firelight.

No one in the bunker down below was talking yet—or if they were, it must have been in whispers meant for other ears than his. He wondered how long it would be until the first dark-suited special agent stepped into the doorway, seeking hostile targets. As it stood, they'd have to hurry up if Worthy would be dueling with the forest adversaries first.

He thought about Tom Altman's auto rifle, but it didn't take a genius to know that going back for it was tantamount to suicide. That left his PSG1 sniper's rifle to repel invaders, plus his Mark 23 pistol with a laser aiming module mounted underneath its barrel. Counting all his magazines, Worthy had one hundred eighty shots before he had to fall back on the frag grenades he wore clipped to his combat webbing.

"Shit," he told himself. "It could be worse, yo."

Knowing it could be a damned sight better, too.

Fighting on two fronts simultaneously was what he'd had in mind for Laurel Lodge, but maybe there was something he could do up front to shave the odds.

Head cocked and listening beside the open door that led outside, Worth unhooked one of his frag grenades, withdrew its pin, and tossed the lethal orb downstairs, hearing it bounce twice from the concrete steps while someone shouted out a warning.

That had been a woman's voice, no doubt—one of the presidential daughters or a female Secret Service agent posted with the sisters just in case one of them had to use the little girl's room or whatever. The grenade went off and someone screamed, a man that time, the shockwave jolting Worthy as it blew a gust of smoke and hot air through the bunker's shattered access doorway.

He supposed it must have been the blast that made him miss the sound of running feet, mounting the porch and coming through the open exit to the world outside. Fabius tried to bring his rifle up, but found his arms no longer followed orders from his brain.

It took another second for him to discover that a woman stood above him, two men crowding in behind her from the moonlit night outside. The woman had an SR-16 carbine leveled at his face. Her lips were moving but he couldn't understand what she was saying.

Grinning like a lunatic, Fabius said, "Looks like you got me, yo, before his world went black.

CHAPTER 12

Dogwood Cabin

"Will you have a seat before you wear holes in the carpet?" James Corbett asked, making no effort to disguise his sarcasm.

Whit Jones stopped pacing for a moment, glared at Corbett, then beheld the DVI's three agents eyeing him and grudgingly sat down.

"This isn't what I signed up for," the White House chief of staff told his small audience.

"Yet, here you are," Corbett reminded him. "And going nowhere fast."

"Why don't you state the obvious?" Jones asked.

As nonelected government officials, serving at the president's pleasure, Jones and Corbett rated only a two-man Secret Service guard detail. Both of those agents were still upstairs, surveilling various approaches to the cabin by moonlight. The bunker's inside team consisted of three former field agents, now serving with the Company's Security Protective Service, who guarded Corbett while he traveled, hard-eyed operators with a history of violence the CIA condoned, while keeping all their exploits strictly classified.

Corbett had hand-picked each of them, providing salary incentives for the nursemaid job such men of action would have turned down had he given them a choice. They might not like the job, but they would still lay down their lives on his behalf, and they came well prepared.

All three were armed with Colt Commando carbines, which they'd brought into Camp David tucked inside of duffel bags. The carbines featured collapsible stocks and 11.5-inch barrels, feeding 5.56×45mm NATO from a variety of STANAG magazines. While lighter and more compact than the parent M16A2 assault rifle, Commando's had the same 950 rounds per minute cyclic rate on full auto, with 550 yards declared as their effective range.

For backup, each SPS operative wore a Glock 21 pistol chambered in .45 ACP, with thirteen rounds in the magazine and one in the chamber. Each also had a second sidearm hidden somewhere on his person, selected individually with the sole proviso that officers qualify with them semiannually, on the shooting range at Langley's George Bush Center for Intelligence.

Corbett himself, while normally unarmed, had cadged a spare Glock 21 from one of his protectors, drawing comfort from its lethal weight tucked underneath his belt.

"We're reasonably safe here," Corbett told his nervous

fellow bunker occupant.

"It doesn't feel that way," Whit Jones replied.

On paper, Jones's job description called for him to select and supervise key White House staffers, control the daily flow of Oval Office visitors, negotiate with Congress and extra-governmental political groups to advance The Man's political agenda, and to generally "protect the president's interests".

For that, he banked $180,000 yearly—your tax dollars at work.

Tonight, though—make that morning now, given the hour—Jones didn't seem capable of sorting paperclips, much less serving the POTUS as his eyes and ears. He might be tough when talking to the media, but when the chips were down, like now, Corbett regarded him with thinly veiled disdain.

After another moment's silence, Jones declared, "I should be with the president, not sitting here."

"He's got enough to think about right now," Corbett replied, "without holding your hand."

"Goddamn it, Jim!"

"Be serious. What could you do for him that can't be done faster and better by his Secret Service detail?"

"It's my job!"

"Okay, then, go."

Jones blinked at him in obvious surprise as Corbett called his bluff. Most bureaucrats in Washington would rather leap from the Statue of Freedom on top of the Capitol dome than get their hands dirty with physical action. Their idea of a workout was turning out for their respective parties' yearly softball games.

"What did you say?" asked Jones, his facial expression stuck somewhere between shock and outrage.

"You heard me, Whit. If you believe the president can't get along without you, go. You know the way to Alpine Lodge. I'm sure one of my men can spare a weapon for you to protect yourself."

"For God's sake, Corbett!"

"No. For *your* sake, Whit. For mine, and everyone around you. We may have out hands full any time now, fighting to survive. I'd rather not be tripping over you or hearing any more complaints."

Jones seemed about to answer, then apparently thought better of it, slumping back into his chair and glowering at Corbett from across the room.

After a silent moment, Corbett spoke again. "All right, then. If you're staying with us, bear in mind that any time now, we may wind up fighting for our lives. Here's what we need to do."

Cesar da Costa liked to work alone whenever possible. Although he had distinguished himself with Brazil's 1st Special Forces Battalion, earning his homeland's Combat Cross First Class and Blood Of Brazil Medal for wounds suffered in combat, da Costa still preferred it when commanders left him to his own devices, trusting him to make them proud.

Tonight, therefore, he was delighted to approach Camp David's Dogwood Cabin with no backup other than the weapons and explosives he was carrying.

Granted, his targets were not on a par with President Martin Harwood or Israeli Prime Minister Jairus Abramson, but da Costa would gladly settle for executing Harwood's chief of staff and his director of the CIA. He'd come prepared for anything, expecting stiff resistance from the Secret Service and the Company's Security Protective Service, but he would not falter.

He would not permit himself to fail.

And when he'd finished his appointed task, had exfiltrated from the president's retreat, a cool one million dollars would be waiting for him in his numbered savings account at Banco Bradesco in Osasco, São Paulo. With wise investments, Cesar reckoned the payoff would last him nicely during the remainder of his life.

But first, he needed to complete his scheduled rendezvous with Death.

Armed with a Mark 18 CQBR/M203 combo, plus a Taurus PT92 9×19mm Parabellum single action/double action pistol manufactured at a former Beretta factory in São Paulo. That explained the sidearm's close resemblance to a Beretta 92, both in appearance and function, but with seventeen rounds in its magazine rather than fifteen. Two extra rounds for one hundred dollars less than the Beretta, and what could possibly go wrong?

Unless, of course, da Costa wound up dead.

Senhor Blair had informed da Costa that his targets were what Blair called "second string," and thus shadowed by fewer guards than Abramson or Harwood, but Blair's goal was a clean sweep of all Camp David's occupants. Da Costa didn't know who was behind the contract, and he did not care.

Too much knowledge could prove more dangerous than not enough.

Da Costa didn't mind a halfway easy job, as long as he received the same payoff as every other member of Blair's team.

Besides his firearms and a Brazilian Armed Forces fighting knife patterned after the U.S. Marine Corps' Ka-Bar, da Costa carried a variety of 40mm grenades for his M203 launcher, M-67 antipersonnel grenades, and Model 308-1 Napalm grenades employed by U.S. Navy SEALs. Toss in a few blocks of C-4 plastique with yards of detonating cord, and he was good to go.

Beginning now.

***

Although he had been half expecting it, the first explosion shocked Whit Jones and brought him to his feet, eyeing the bunker's feroconcrete ceiling overhead.

"They're here!" he blurted out, regretting it immediately, shooting glances at Jim Corbett and his lackeys to find out if they were staring at him, judging Jones to be a coward and a fool.

His own resolve hardened after the second blast upstairs, his mind flashing, *To hell with what they think.*

"There goes our Secret Service team," said Corbett.

Jones spoke without thinking. "What? How do you know that?"

"Use your head," Corbett replied, dismissively. "Did you see either of them carrying explosives?"

"No, but—"

"But nothing. Somebody took them out before they had a chance to fire."

As if in answer to the DCI's pronouncement, a short burst of automatic weapon's fire rattled and echoed from the general direction of the upstairs kitchen.

"And there went the *coup de grâce*," said Corbett.

Looking at him, Whit Jones couldn't tell whether the DCI was troubled by two agents being murdered, of if he took satisfaction at the vindication of his former dire prediction.

Turning toward his stoic bodyguards, Jones told them, "You're up, gentlemen. Nobody makes it down the stairs. You understand?"

"Yes sir," they answered him, almost as one.

"Still not too late to arm yourself," Corbett told Jones.

Embarrassed, nearly certain he was blushing, Jones replied, "I've never fired a weapon in my life."

Corbett regarded Jones as if he were a worm revealed by flipping over mossy stones.

"Not even when you were a kid?" the DCI inquired. "A twenty-two? Maybe a pellet gun?"

"Nothing." Jones felt his shoulders slump as he replied.

There seemed no point in adding that his parents had been founding members of the Brady Campaign to Prevent Gun Violence. That would only make them view him as less of a "man".

Well, screw them.

Corbett was saying, "Eric, can you hook him up?"

"Yes, sir!" The former spook turned bodyguard, identified by Corbett as one Eric Stanhope in their round of introductions, reached under his jacket and removed a compact pistol with a satin stainless finish, handing it to Jones. The White House chief of staff accepted it reluctantly, guessing its weight at twelve or thirteen ounces.

"That's a Colt Mustang," Stanhope explained. "It takes .380 ACP rounds, six inside the magazine, one in the chamber. If you need to use it, bear in mind the first shot's single-action."

"Meaning what?" Jones asked.

"You need to cock the hammer with your thumb before you aim and pull the trigger. Squeeze it, don't jerk, or else you likely won't hit anything. After the first shot, it will cock itself. The slide locks open when it's empty and you need to switch out magazines."

"Do you have any more?" Jones asked.

"Sorry. It's strictly backup for the carbine and the Glock. If you've hit nothing after seven shots," Stanhope concluded with a shrug, "you probably won't have to think about reloading."

"Right," said Jones, while thinking, *Thanks so bloody much.*

"Okay, then," said DCI Corbett. "We need to hold the access door and stairs, or else we're history. Whit, stand off to my left here."

Jones stood on the spot Corbett had indicated, eyes locked on the steel door shutting off the basement stairs.

"What now?" he asked.

"If anyone comes through the door, blast him, unless you recognize him as a Secret Service agent."

"And that's all?" asked Jones.

"Just one more thing," Corbett replied. "Try not to shoot me in the ass."

So far, Cesar da Costa didn't think the Secret Service men he'd faced were all that propaganda made them out to be.

They'd been professional, of course, well-armed, presumably well trained at taking care of politicians who were mostly egomaniacs and often fools, but neither of the agents left to guard the ground floor of Camp David's Dogwood Cabin had come close to stopping him.

That came as no surprise to Cesar. They were only *policiais*, though exalted ones, and thus could not expect to best da Costa's training or his battlefield experience.

And to be fair, he had surprised them outset with a dose of shock and awe.

The first round he had triggered from his M203 launcher was an M433 HEDP grenade—its designation short for "high-explosive dual-purpose". It improved on HEAT rounds—"high-explosive anti-tank" munitions—by surrounding the warhead with a conventional fragmentation casing, thereby improving blast and fragmentation attacks on unarmored targets.

One such had been Dogwood Cabin's front door.

Immediately after blowing that door off its hinges, hurling it across the darkened room within, da Costa had reloaded with a basic HE round, rocking the cabin from its attic down to its foundation, at least briefly stunning anyone on the ground floor.

In fact, as he had soon discovered, the initial HEDP round had killed one of the cabin's watchmen outright, riddling him with shrapnel and long slivers from the stout front door before he knew what had befallen him.

The second 40mm round had not quite finished off the second Secret Service guard, but he was clearly dazed and gasping when da Costa greased him with a short burst from his automatic carbine.

After that, nothing remained but sweeping through the vacant, smoky rooms to satisfy Cesar that no one had been overlooked. That done, he could assault the Dogwood bunker and eliminate whoever might be hiding down below.

For that, he had to choose between a HEAT grenade or C-4, swiftly making up his mind to try the 40mm first.

HEAT rounds employ the "Munroe effect", pioneered in the late 18th century and modified in recent times to penetrate thick vehicular armor. Boiled down to basics, the rounds function by having their explosive charge collapse a metal liner inside the warhead into a high-velocity superplastic jet, wherein solid crystalline material is deformed well beyond its usual breaking point—2,000 percent on average—and causing that jet to pierce armor seven times thicker than the initial projectile's diameter.

The net result: a heavy tank—or a bunker secured by an armored door—became a slaughter pen of fire and shrapnel ripping wires, machinery and furniture or human flesh to shreds.

Of course, that didn't mean da Costa's next round would annihilate his enemies hiding downstairs. Most likely, he'd be facing stairs and yet another door below, but if a HEAT round blew the first door, he could use a second to the same end.

After that, it all came down to mopping up, then moving on to other targets in the compound.

One way or another, Cesar planned to make this night his last one on the firing line.

And to that end, he might as well run up a record body count.

"It won't be long now," DCI Corbett advised his four companions in the Dogwood Cabin's bunker. "Stand your ground and give 'em everything you've got."

He glanced over at Whit Jones, to his left, noting that Jones's hands were trembling where they gripped the borrowed Colt Mustang. Not good for target acquisition, but at least Jones had remembered to cock the .380's hammer and hadn't fired it accidentally while doing so.

And if he died down there, perhaps Jones would go out feeling that he'd done something to repel their unknown enemies.

The life he'd led in politics, always a "me-too" guy bound to someone of higher rank and influence, maybe that was the best Jones could expect as he approached his private end of days.

The firefight overhead had wound up being swift and final, no major resistance from the Secret Service duo stationed on the cabin's ground floor. Corbett took for granted that the agents there were dead. Nothing he'd heard during the brief skirmish suggested that they'd done any damage to Camp David's enemies.

Where were the reinforcements from outside? Corbett no longer harbored any realistic hope that they'd arrive in time to save the day, although with any luck, at least the president might manage to survive.

As far as Dogwood Cabin went, Corbett hoped that he would be able to dispatch at least one of the raiders who had put to shame America's defense of its commanding officer.

Upstairs, a blast much louder than the first two rocked the cabin down to its foundation. Something bulky, ponderous, came crashing down the access stairs and slammed into the door Corbett was covering, backed by his agents and the White House chief of staff.

"One door down," he announced. "And one more left to go."

Corbett thought he was prepared for anything, but he was startled when the lower level's access door absorbed an ear-numbing explosion, pierced by what appeared to be a stream of molten metal from outside. That flame enveloped one of his defenders, Agent David Flannery, and left him shrieking as he rolled around the bunker's floor, his fellow operatives whipping off their coats and flailing at the hungry fire.

"Get back!" the DCI commanded them, but neither listened or obeyed him in their rush of panic. Realizing they had passed beyond control, he barked at Jones, "Stand ready! Anything can happen now!"

And so it did.

From somewhere in the corridor or on the stairs beyond the bunker's ruptured door, an enemy began to fire short bursts of automatic fire inside, using the blown-out entrance as a gun port. Within seconds flat, incoming rounds struck Agents Stanhope and Bob Dickerson, both collapsing to the bunker's nubby indoor-outdoor carpeting.

Corbett couldn't have said if either operative was alive or dead, and he had no time to consider it just now. Clutching his Glock 21 in a two-handed grip, he stood off-center from the "bombproof" door and snapped at Jones to join him, sheltered briefly from the hostile gunman's line of fire.

That wouldn't last, Corbett assumed. A few more bursts would send wild ricochets caroming off the bunker's feroconcrete walls, trapping the DCI and his White House companion in a crazy, lethal pinball game.

Corbett could only hope that he would get a clear shot at his enemies, maybe take one of them along with him into the never-ending dark before he died.

Cesar da Costa pressed his CQBR's magazine release catch, dropped the empty mag, and slapped a fully loaded thirty-round replacement into the Mark 18's magazine well. It snapped into place and he cocked the carbine's charging handle, counting backwards down from ten as he prepared to charge inside the bunker.

It was risky, granted, both the possibility of gunfire from within and fear that he might snag his camouflage fatigues while ducking through the jagged vent his HEAT grenade had blasted in the bunker's access door.

Risky—but what else could da Costa do to guarantee that he'd eliminated everyone hiding inside?

Unless…

He palmed one of his frag grenades, removed its safety pin and pitched it underhand into the room his 40mm round had breached. Cesar ducked backward and off to his left, counting the seconds down until a blast echoed inside the bunker and he heard the pinging sound of steel fragments rebounding from its inner walls.

More smoke came drifting through the shattered entryway. Da Costa stood and strained his ears to catch the barest hint of movement on the far side of the violated portal. Close to a full minute passed before he eased up to the entryway and poked his carbine's muzzle through, waiting to see if he drew fire.

So far, so good.

It felt like now or never to da Costa as he edged forward, then ducked his head to clear the vent produced by his HEAT round, its edges hot enough to scorch him still, as one steel prong grazed Cesar's scalp.

"*Maldito inferno!*" he cursed, recoiling from the sudden pain. "*Filho de uma cadela maldita!*"

When no one answered him, or questioned what he'd said, da Costa felt relieved. Perhaps his basement targets were all dead, in fact—or, at the very least, stunned into semi-consciousness, their ear drums perforated.

There was no time better than the present to find out.

In front of Cesar as he entered, three men lay clustered together on the blackened carpeting. Bullets or shrapnel from his frag grenade had punctured them erratically, between their shoulders and their thighs, blood streaming from those wounds. Additionally, one of them was badly burned, his suit still smoldering, ignited by the white-hot superplastic jet from Cesar's second HEAT grenade.

No danger there, that he could see. Da Costa wasted no more ammunition on the three defenders who were either dead or well along their way.

Cesar turned to his right, saw no one lurking there, then swiveled to his left, where two dazed-looking men sat on the floor, reclining with their backs against a tattered, smoking couch.

Approaching to within six feet of him, his index finger on the CQBR's trigger, Cesar stooped and peered at them more closely, trying to discover what felt wrong to him about their posture or their attitude.

Too late, he saw the pistols each man clutched in his right hand.

DCI James Corbett was reclining with his eyes closed, stunned and hurting, when he heard someone enter the bunker, moving cautiously. Beside him, Whit Jones shifted slightly, moaned, and then slumped back as if the effort was too much for him.

A few more seconds, Corbett thought. *Just come a little closer, asshole.*

When he heard a boot scuff on the bunker's tattered carpet, barely two yards distant from him by the sound of it, Corbett opened his eyes, beheld his enemy, and said, "Nice you could make it."

As the slim, Hispanic-looking man in winter camouflage fatigues recoiled, raising hit automatic rifle, Corbett thrust his Glock out to arm's length in front of him and fired as rapidly as he could squeeze its trigger. Growling in his throat—a fierce, involuntary sound—he didn't notice Whit Jones joining in until the echoes from his borrowed Colt Mustang stung Corbett's ears.

The soldier who'd been bent on killing them reeled backward as a burst of .380 and .45 ACP slugs ripped into him, spilling bright crimson blood from holes appearing in his mottled camo jacket. Corbet raised his pistol, fired one shot into the falling gunman's face, and saw an eye burst from its socket, airborne off to who knew where.

Both Jones and Corbett kept on firing till the slides locked open on their pistols, curls of smoke emerging from the empty, open chambers. In spite of that, Jones tried to keep on firing, spewing curses when his gun refused to play along.

"Enough!" said Corbett, reaching out with his left hand and pushing down Whit's shooting hand. "He's done. We're empty, damn it!"

"Is he dead?" Jones gasped.

"I hope so," Corbett answered. "If he's not, I promise you he'll be pissed off."

Jones laughed at that, but Corbett couldn't tell of he felt sweet relief or else was verging on hysteria.

Whatever. They still faced a threat from other enemies and had to get a move on if they hoped to make it out alive.

"Get up," he ordered Jones, surprised when Whit obeyed and actually moved faster than Corbett, rising from the floor.

"What can we do about the others?" Jones inquired.

After a closer look at his three fallen agents, Corbett answered with a question of his own. "You're not a trauma surgeon, are you?"

"What? Of course, not."

"Then we can't do anything. Between their gunshot wounds and shrapnel, piled on top of Stanhope's burns, they're either dead already or will be within the next few minutes."

"So, we just run off and leave them here like this?"

"No," Corbett replied, pulling the reins back on a surge of anger. "First, we don't go *running off* to anywhere. Camp David's still in hostile hands, as far as I know, and quickest way I know to wind up dead is wandering around outside."

"So, you just want to stay down here with them? Waiting until somebody else comes by to finish us?"

"Did I say that?" When Jones made no reply, the DCI answered his own question. "No, I did not."

"What, then?"

"First, we pick up any weapons we can salvage, then we slip out quietly and have a look around. From there on out, we're playing it by ear."

***

Whit Jones felt trapped inside a nightmare that resisted all attempts to wake himself and shake it off. If anyone had told him this would be the climax of his visit to Camp David, he would probably have laughed at them—or phoned for psychiatric intervention.

Still, he followed Corbett's orders, helping the Director of Central Intelligence disarm their dead enemy. The corpse yielded an automatic rifle, a sidearm, plus extra ammunition magazines and hand grenades of disparate shapes and sizes.

Setting those weapons aside, they moved on to the doubly repugnant task of recovering pistols and more magazines from the CIA men who had died defending their director.

Four more pistols there, with extra ammunition, added to their stash while imagined one of Corbett's men was moaning softly, hitching ragged breaths.

"All right," Jones said. "What now?"

"I'm guessing that you've never fired a CQBR," Corbett said.

"Whatever that means," Jones replied.

"My point, exactly. So, I'll take the rifle and two pistols, right? You grab as many handguns as you reckon you can carry. Keep one in your hand, and tuck at least one other in your belt."

Jones followed through mechanically, still wondering if he was fully conscious after all that he'd been through.

"And the grenades?" he asked Corbett.

"They'd come in handy," his companion granted. "Sure, why not? I'll stuff a couple of them in my pockets, just in case."

Jones didn't mind being discouraged from collecting hand grenades. The way he felt right now, he'd likely pull one of their pins by accident and blow himself to bloody smithereens.

"What now?" Jones asked Corbett.

"Now, we get out of here," the DCI replied. "But carefully, okay? With any luck, we'll run into marines or Secret Service agents hunting for the infiltrators. Just be sure you don't go off half-cocked and take a shot at any friendlies."

Jones didn't reply to that. He took for granted that any marines they met prowling around Camp David ought to be in uniform, the Secret Service agents wearing business garb. Jones knew he didn't truly qualify as any kind of soldier, but he'd helped to kill a man and figured he was smart enough to tell the difference between killers in winter camouflage and those Corbett was calling "friendlies".

But would that be adequate on such a night as this, by moonlight, when defenders of the presidential compound spotted men they might not recognize, armed to the teeth? What would prevent a squad of leathernecks or Secret Service agencies cutting loose on him and DCI Corbett if one group took the other by surprise?

Nothing at all, Jones thought, *except dumb luck.*

Until sunrise, survival at Camp David would remain a crapshoot, and he wasn't sure that even daybreak would relieve the risk. As long as enemies were prowling through the presidential compound's woods, no one was truly safe.

Jones had two pistols now, together with spare magazines which Corbett had assured him were the proper size and caliber. Neither looked very much like the Colt Mustang he had fired into his one and only human target, but he guessed their operating principles were similar.

You point and squeeze the trigger, after making sure the safety catch was in its "OFF" position. Beyond that, Jones remained a total novice, understanding that he had neither the time nor spare ammo to gain a measure of proficiency.

Climbing the basement stairs, they came to Dogwood Cabin's dark ground floor. The stench of cordite and explosives nearly nauseated Jones—a feeling that increased once they had found their former Secret Service watchmen lying dead and drenched with blood.

That made five men who'd died protecting him tonight, and Jones couldn't help wondering if he was worth their sacrifice.

As they proceeded toward the porch, his mind kicked in again, to ward off bleak depression.

Was he worth the cost of keeping him alive?

I'd goddamned better be, Jones thought.

CHAPTER 13

Holly Cabin

"What is it like out there," Prime Minister Jairus Abramson asked the chief of his Mossad security detail.

Naftali Sharett, just back from a cautious scouting tour of the woods surrounding Holly Cabin thought about his answer for a moment before speaking. "Sir," he said, "I heard less firing on the grounds than previously, but it's clear no reinforcements have arrived so far. When that occurs, we should expect large numbers of them, certainly with bullhorns, probably with armored vehicles."

"And what do you surmise from their delay?" the older man inquired.

"I tried my cell phone once I got topside," said Sharett. "Likewise, the same thing with my walkie-talkie. The invaders still are jamming all communications channels."

"So, the outside world may not yet be aware of our predicament," said Abramson, his observation not phrased as a question.

Sharett felt obliged to answer anyway. "No, sir. But from the protocol that was explained to me, the Secret Service should have noted the persistent failure to report on schedule. Measures should be underway by now, satellite imaging to start, perhaps an overflight by helicopter."

"But you heard no aircraft passing over?" Abramson pressed his subordinate.

"No, sir. Nothing."

"But you encountered none of the attackers."

"No, sir. All the shots I heard were farther off. I thought it was too dangerous, tracking those sounds to learn what's happening. But if you wish..."

The PM stopped him short. "No, no. You've risked too much already. If we leave, it must be as a group. Together we might stand a chance."

Abramson wished that he believed himself.

"Sir, if you'll allow me to advise you..."

"It is your duty, Captain, as my duty is to listen."

"Thank you, sir. I'm not convinced that we should leave this place to roam about the compound. It seems to me that you are an intended target of this paramilitary action, possibly *the* target. To expose you further is, I think, unwise."

"And are we safer waiting here, Captain? Even downstairs, inside the bunker, we have heard explosions. Should our enemies arrive with weapons capable of breaching our security..."

"Yes, sir. I understand. But even so, I still prefer imperfect cover to attempting an escape with none at all."

Abramson nodded. Said, "I quite agree, and wonder whether we are even able to escape the compound as it stands. With our communications jammed, may not the gates be likewise? If we reached them, could we scale the fence in time to keep from being caught and shot?"

"I would not try the gates, Prime Minister," Sharett replied. "With the electric power cut and gunmen on the prowl, I must discourage any such attempt."

"But if we tried it, Captain, what do you suppose might be our chances of success?"

"It's difficult to say, sir. If I had to guess, I might say odds of two-to-one that we shall not survive."

"Or, put another way, one out of three chances for ultimate success."

Sharett allowed himself a shrug. "I can't say 'ultimate success,' sir. I would have to break the odds down in accordance without number versus that of our opponents."

"Yes, yes." Abramson fanned one hand in the air between them, as if sweeping Sharett's argument away. "But we *might* make it."

"To the gate, it's possible. I won't deny it sir. *Beyond* the gate and fence to safety, I believe the odds are heavier against us."

"I'm convinced that we should try it, Captain."

"Sir—"

Before Sharett could press his point, one of the other Mossad agents called out from the cabin's front windows. "Someone's approaching, sir. He's wearing camouflage and has an automatic weapon."

Abramson immediately felt his shoulders sag.

"And now," he told Sharett, "it seems we are too late."

***

Dion O'Reilly could see flashlight beams bobbing around behind the curtains drawn across the Holly Cabin's windows. They cast shadows in the forms of skulking men with guns.

The former Irish Army Ranger was a bit surprised to find the cabin's ground floor occupied. He'd been expecting any occupants to be below ground, tucked inside the feroconcrete shelter that was standard at Camp David for all buildings occupied by guests and staff. What could his targets have in mind, avoiding shelter down below?

Perhaps he'd stumbled on a clutch of claustrophobes, although that seemed preposterous. More likely, they had been downstairs a while, but then decided they'd be better off to make a break for it.

"Thank god for idiots," O'Reilly muttered to himself, and shifted his grip on the PSG1 sniper's rifle he was carrying. Ideally, if he waited for a bit, O'Reilly thought his quarry might emerge onto the cabin's moonlit porch, where he could pick them off with ease. And failing that, perhaps they would desist from their erratic walking back and forth behind the curtains, giving him a chance to fix his weapon's Hensoldt ZF telescopic sight on one or more of them.

Like shooting ducks frozen onto an icy pond, O'Reilly thought, and smiled.

He sat down with his back against the rough bark of a tall oak tree, knees raced to serve him as a makeshift gun rest. Shouldering his rifle, peered through its scope toward the cabin, watching shadows move behind the drapes.

From fifty yards, O'Reilly knew that he could drill a moving target, but the window glass and curtains might divert his bullet, throwing it off-course enough to only wound his chosen prey, perhaps to miss the target altogether.

And he'd learned from long experience that sniper fire had much in common with a first impression. Namely, you could only make a good one on your first attempt.

And after that...

Whoever was assigned to Holly Cabin, he assumed they would have armed guards in attendance, all with weapons at the ready now, with an invasion of Camp David under way. Defenders of the cabin would find it more difficult to drop O'Reilly than his own fire headed their way ought to be.

For starters, none of them could even glimpse him unless they first drew back the curtains, which would leave the cabin's occupants exposed. That, plus the difficulty of a man inside even a dimly lighted room, scanning the night outside, meant the defenders could not trust their own night vision.

To wait or forge ahead; that was the question.

And he thought, *To hell with it.*

O'Reilly stretched out prone, snow crunching under him as he got reasonably comfortable, lining up his shot. First thing, he unfolded the rifle's bipod, let its twenty-six-inch barrel stabilize, half of the weapon's sixteen pounds transferred from Dion's hands onto the brace that came as standard from the Heckler & Koch factory.

O'Reilly took a deep breath, then released approximately half of it and held the rest, immediately conscious of his own pulse throbbing in his ears, beneath the soft ballistic plugs. The stock's vertically adjustable cheek pad was cold against his face, and that was fine.

He tracked the cabin's moving shadows for another sixty seconds, give or take, then stroked the PSG1's trigger, felt the rifle's pivoting butt cap recoil against his shoulder as 147 grains of sudden death flew down range, traveling 930 yards per second toward impact.

Baltimore

Thaddeus Resnikoff was starting to become concerned.

Despite all that he knew about security around Camp David, and provisions for suppressing—or at least delaying—any news broadcasts concerning trouble there, he had expected some reports to leak by now.

Resnikoff checked his Rolex Cosmograph Daytona Men's Black Dial watch for the third time in the past half-hour, frowning time displayed. He could not blame the wristwatch, which had cost him $27,999—presumably some advertising asshole's notion of a joke, as if one dollar made a difference—

since he had changed its battery just yesterday.

"Proklyatyy sukin syn!" he cursed, and then repeated it for emphasis, as if he could somehow impress his empty flat.

If anything was wrong, if the assault had been delayed somehow, he should have heard from Blair at once. If law enforcement officers had intercepted Blair's team on arrival, prior to penetration of the president's retreat, there should have been a bulletin on CNN once the arrests were made.

What, then?

Worry did not suit Resnikoff. It made him agitated, restless, with a tendency to do things he regretted later. Thankfully, tonight he was alone, no one to watch him or to ask him idiotic questions about how he felt, what he was thinking, blah-blah-blah.

That could have been the last straw, tipping him over the edge to homicide.

If something had gone wrong, Resnikoff's final payment was in jeopardy. Worse yet, his sponsors for this mission—certain major players from the House of Saud, collaborating with a leader of the German Nationalistische Volkspartei—would not, of course, be satisfied to simply withhold payment of the money they owed Resnikoff. They would demand a refund of their large down payment, long since spent, and would undoubtedly attempt to silence him for good.

That had been tried before, on more than one occasion, but with such resources at their fingertips, Resnikoff knew the task of killing him would be entrusted to elite professionals. And while he had his own hired guns on tap for such emergencies, he understood the clear and present danger of his current situation.

Failure, at that level of the game, was absolutely unacceptable.

The arms dealer began to check his watch again but stopped himself. His four large flat-screen televisions were all set to different news channels, volume turned down low, the images enough to warn him if a SPECIAL BULLETIN was broadcast from London, New York City, Lyon, or from Doha, in Qatar.

If bad news broke, his private jet was standing by, already fueled and ready for immediate departure out of Baltimore/ Washington International Thurgood Marshal Airport. First, though, before Resnikoff took that irrevocable step, he had a call to make.

His party picked up on the second ring, a voice he recognized skipping the usual preliminaries, asking him, "What's wrong?"

"Perhaps nothing," said Resnikoff. "But just in case…"

"Yes? What?"

"Your bag is packed, I take it?"

"Shit!" A heartbeat's hesitation, then, "It's ready, yes."

"All right. Stay where you are. I'll be in touch."

✳✳✳

Holly Cabin, Camp David

Jairus Abramson was in the cabin's kitchen, opening a bottle of Goldstar Dark Lager, the only beer he drank, when he was suddenly distracted by a sharp *crack* from the living room, immediately followed by the *thud* of someone dropping to the floor.

The echo of a rifle shot from somewhere in the woods outside came a split-second later, overriding curses from Abramson's bodyguards.

Shielded from line of sight to any of the cabin's windows, the prime minister replaced his Goldstar bottle in the kitchen's Whirlpool side-by-side refrigerator—there was no point wasting it—and made his cautious way back toward the living room. Before he got there, yet another shot punched through one of the windows, spraying glass around the room, ending its flight inside one of the stucco walls.

Dropping to hands and knees, Abramson called out to his men, "Is everyone all right?"

Captain Naftali Sharett's voice came back to him. "No, sir. Stay where you are and out of sight!"

"Who has been injured?" the prime minister demanded.

"It's Noah, sir. He's dead."

Abramson knew that he should not have been surprised, but even so...

Sergeant Noah Sussman had been part of Abramson's security detail since he became prime minister. He had a wife and four children, ranging in age from twelve to four years old. There would be no solace in hearing that Sussman had died defending someone they had never met, but only watched on television broadcasts.

Pushing those thoughts out of mind, Abramson asked Captain Sharett, "How many shooters are there?"

"I believe it's only one, sir. Firing through the drapes, it had to be a lucky shot, but if it happened once…"

"I understand. He must be stopped."

"Yes, sir. I'll go out through the back myself and try to come around behind him."

Abramson considered that, then answered back, "No, Captain. Stay there with your men."

"But, sir—"

"You have your order, Captain. Please acknowledge."

"Yes, sir. As you say, sir. But I hope you won't—"

Abramson did not hear the rest of it. He was already moving, taking long strides toward the cabin's backdoor, tuning out the protests from his captain of security. He drew the borrowed Jericho 941 semiauto pistol from under his belt, checking the "Baby Eagle" as it had been dubbed in advertisements, confirming that the gun's combined safety/decocking lever had been set to "OFF," the piece ready to fire if he depressed its double-action trigger.

A blast of cold air struck Abramson as he cleared the cabin's exit, latching the backdoor behind him. At that same moment, another rifle shot rang out, erasing his regret at failing to retrieve his topcoat from the bedroom he had occupied. Anger would have to warm Abramson now, as he stepped off through pallid moonlight, circling around the length of Holly Cabin to pursue his enemy.

Southwest of Alpine Lodge

Nick Blair was on his own and on the prowl.

He had dispersed his soldiers following the barracks massacre, retreating to the role of supervisor for the ultimate annihilation of Camp David. In the past hour and change, he'd heard sporadic gunfire echoing from various locations in the compound, coupled with explosions that suggested his team was proceeding as commanded—but in truth, he couldn't say if they were on the verge of triumph or defeat.

That was a problem, with communications jammed on every frequency. Blair couldn't stay in touch with his commandos, checking on their progress or their losses in the field, except by personal contact at great risk to himself.

That didn't stop him, though. Blair lived for risk, for the excitement that it generated and the satisfaction he derived from any job well done.

Of course, he also lived for cash, and if his men failed to deliver on their contract with Thad Resnikoff, none of them would receive another dime for this night's work.

In fact, they would be lucky to survive.

Blair had contingencies in place, of course. He never undertook a mission without planning well ahead for his survival and escape. His record was exemplary, but logic told him everyone ran out of luck at some point in their lives. That might mean temporary unemployment, maybe even homelessness for some.

In Blair's case, though, the consequence of failure would

be death.

Unless, that was, he managed to reach Resnikoff before the arms dealer dispatched fresh hunters to erase all record of his bold conspiracy.

As Blair approached the president's retreat, hoping to find it leveled and in ashes, a pervasive smell of smoke initially encouraged him. It took a bit more time for him to make out Aspen Lodge by moonlight and to realize that it remained intact.

He could see damage from explosions, where his mercenaries had initiated their assault, but there should have been more. Much more, in fact. From what he saw now—crumpled, bloodstained figures clad in winter camouflage fatigues—that someone, somehow, had derailed at least this crucial portion of his plan.

Blair doubted that the Secret Service could have picked them off. Despite their preparation at the Federal Law Enforcement Training Center in Glynco, Georgia, Blair did not believe that any gung-ho feds could beat his soldiers in a standup fight—much less covert maneuvers in a forest setting.

No.

Somebody else must be responsible, but who? And how many?

One thing was certain, peering through the trees at Alpine Lodge. Blair didn't want to meet the warriors who had topped his own and left them sprawled in pools of swiftly cooling blood.

Only one question now remained. Should he continue on

his rounds, check out more targets from his hit list, or accept that he was up shit's creek without the proverbial paddle?

Whatever he decided, Blair knew that he must choose soon, and exercise great caution as he made his next critical move.

He'd stop by Laurel Lodge next, and if that turned out to be a bust, to hell with it. Blair didn't plan to wait around for any stragglers from his strike team to appear, then exfiltrate himself along with them.

They'd known from day one that the mission could turn out to be their last. That's why Thad Resnikoff had offered up a million dollars each to see it through, with half paid out up front. The prick would likely want a refund if they failed, but he could take that up with Blair next time they saw each other.

Right, Blair thought, and smiled. *Unless I see you first, asshole.*

In which case there'd be one less scumbag arms dealer to multiply Earth's misery.

And who would even miss him, after all?

✳✳✳

Holly Cabin

Dion O'Reilly paused to scan the cabin through Olympus Tracker 12x25 Compact Binoculars, giving his eyes a rest from the Hensoldt ZF rifle scope.

He'd pumped eight rounds into the cabin's windows, leaving twelve shots in his magazine, but after the first hit, O'Reilly doubted that he'd scored on any of his human targets. That was no surprise, under the circumstances, but he had a hinky feeling now—a kind of sixth sense that he'd found to be a lifesaver in certain combat situations—that forewarned him of approaching danger.

Then again, it might just be a combination of the cold night air and gas from the burritos he'd consumed en route to reach Camp David.

Damn those refried beans with onions, anyhow.

O'Reilly wished he drawn one of the Mark 18 CQBRs, complete with M203 launcher, so that he could light the cabin up with HE and incendiary rounds. That was the surest way to flush its occupants into the open, whereas sniper fire only encouraged them to keep their heads and asses down, well out of sight.

He carried hand grenades, of course, like everybody else on Nick Blair's team, but using them required O'Reilly to advance, expose himself to possible defensive fire. The guys inside there had at least two submachine guns, since he'd seen that many firing through the cabin's shattered windows simultaneously. Neither had come close to tagging him, but that could change if he crawled out from under cover and advanced to start tossing grenades.

The PSG1 was a good weapon for nailing targets at a distance, but it had not been designed for rushing fortified positions when a soldier was outnumbered and outgunned.

O'Reilly's H&K USP pistol could provide covering fire, but once its sixteen rounds had been expended, he'd be stuck in no-man's land, juggling his rifle and a frag grenade while trying to replace the pistol's empty magazine.

And that wasn't what Dion thought of as a sure-fire ticket to success.

More likely, it would get him killed.

No. If he meant to pull it off, he'd have to creep in under cover of the scudding clouds that had obscured the full moon's light, get close enough while moving quietly, then lob at least one frag grenade into the cabin, maybe followed up with na-palm to create the screaming chaos he desired.

And once the occupants were scrambling to escape, then they belonged to him.

He might still earn the money Nick Blair owed to him—that is, if Blair himself were still alive. Since splitting up, O'Reilly didn't have a clue what any other members of the team were doing, whether they'd succeeded at their goals or been cut down and blown away.

Dion knew damned well he wouldn't miss them if they died but escaping from Camp David with his own skin in one piece would be a whole lot easier with backup standing by.

Maybe, if he could take his present target down...

Resigned to it, O'Reilly rose and started creeping forward, rifle in his left hand, with a frag grenade clutched in his right.

His not to reason why, and all that happy crap.

***

"Is it still bleeding?" Sergeant Gershom Dayan asked Captain Sharett.

"No longer, thanks to you," Sharett replied.

"Basic first aid," Dayan reminded his superior. "It's lucky that I wore a tie."

During the first flurry of sniper fire, after Sergeant Sussman was killed, a slug had punched through Captain Sharett's left biceps and nicked his brachial artery, a potentially fatal wound until Dayan whipped off his knit silk tie and used it as a makeshift tourniquet to stop the bleeding.

Both Mossad commandos knew the tourniquet itself was dangerous if left in place too long, potentially producing clots, myonecrosis—also known as "gas gangrene"—acute renal failure, even amputation of the injured limb. To fend off those adverse developments, instructors warned against leaving a tourniquet in place for more than two hours, and minimizing excessive pressure beyond complete blood flow cessation, but a battlefield restricted a first aid suppliers options.

"You may have saved my life, Sergeant," Sharett replied.

"Not yet, sir," Dayan said. "And what of the prime minister?"

"You know his combat record, Gershom."

"And I also know his age, Naftali."

Nodding, Sharett grudgingly acknowledged, "He's a hard man to refuse."

"But if he's killed out there tonight, or incapacitated…"

"Don't remind me. If it comes to that—and God forbid it—I take full responsibility for the decision."

Sergeant Dayan had expected that, knowing the captain as

he did, but guilt still haunted him.

"I wish that we could cover him, at least," he said.

"And who says that we can't?" Sharett replied. "I still have three—no, four—clips for my Uzi, then my pistol."

"I have two full Uzi magazines," Dayan replied, "and one that's down by half."

"If nothing else, we could at least distract the sniper," Captain Sharett said.

"Or even score a lucky hit by accident," Dayan agreed.

Sharett flashed him a brief, pained smile. Said, "In which case, claim we planned it all along."

"Why not?" Dayan replied. "As long as we don't accidentally shoot the prime minister."

"In that case," Sharett said, "I shall remove the tourniquet and you can blame it all on me."

"Don't think I won't," Sergeant Dayan agreed, though both men knew that he would never even dream of doing such a thing.

"All right, then," Captain Sharett said, already scooting toward the shattered windows on his backside, wincing as he slid through broken glass.

Dayan kept pace with his commander, down on hands and knees to keep himself below the outdoor sniper's line of fire.

"You know," he said, "I'll miss Sussman, despite his rotten jokes."

"And bad breath, too," Sharett added.

"Perhaps we can accomplish this for him," Dayan said.

"And for the prime minister," Sharett added.

With nothing more to say, both men lifted their SMGs up to the nearest windowsills and opened fire into the night.

✳✳✳

The moment that he heard two Uzis firing from the cabin, Jairus Abramson knew what his bodyguards were doing, drawing hostile fire in hopes that he could spot the shooter lurking in the woods nearby and finish him.

Israel's prime minister hoped he was worthy of their trust in him and equal to the task.

Mossad did not load Uzi SMGs with tracer rounds, so Abramson could not tell if his two surviving agents had a target in their sights, or if they simply had decided to provide what cover fire they could for his advance. In either case, he hoped they were not wasting ammunition, risking their own lives in vain.

He reached the cabin's southwest corner, peered around it, and was taken by surprise to see a rifleman advancing from the tree line, ducking low and weaving now as automatic fire spat through the air above his head. Disguised in winter camouflage, with no lights beaming from the cabin, there was still a chance that Sharett and Dayan would fail to spot him, most particularly if they stayed below the parlor's windowsills to duck incoming fire.

But Abramson had seen the enemy and had at least a fighting chance to take him down.

Some Jericho 941s came with illuminated night sights, but

the borrowed pistol in his hand bore only fixed sights, meant for use in combat where adjustability allowed for damage and attachments run on batteries could fail when they were needed most. Still...

Kneeling, with the Baby Eagle clutched in a two-handed grip, Abramson tracked his moving target, led the runner by a yard or so, and squeezed the trigger twice, a double tap as he'd been taught in basic training for the IDF. In retrospect, he could not say if either round struck its intended mark, or if the pistol's noise and muzzle flashes simply made the runner break his stride.

In either case, his would-be killer faltered, half-turned toward the sound of pistol fire, and thus presented Abramson with an expanded target for his next two shots in rapid fire. And this time, there could be no doubt that one 9mm round, at least, had ripped into the runner's chest or abdomen.

The camo-clad attacker stumbled, dropped to hands and knees, losing his rifle as he fell. Instead of reaching down for it, however, his right hand came up to breastbone level, while his left crossed over, plucked at something, then his right drew back as if to pitch something in Abramson's direction.

It could only be a hand grenade.

Cursing in Hebrew, Abramson cranked off another double tap and heard the wounded soldier grunt with pain before he toppled over, sprawling on his back. The wounded runner's right hand, raised above his head, was only six or seven inches from his helmet when a blast ripped through the night, its shock wave dropping Abramson facedown into the snow.

When the prime minister rose to all fours and faced his enemy again, the sniper was no longer any threat to anyone—unless, perhaps, some passerby suffered from delicate digestion. Meant to stop small arms fire, his helmet had offered no protection from a close-range frag grenade's explosion ripping through his face, shoulders and neck, nearly decapitating him.

Abramson waited a few more seconds, hoping no one else would charge out of the snowy woods, then struggled to his feet and called out to his men inside the cabin. "Captain Sharett! Sergeant Dayan! I think it may be safe to come outside."

CHAPTER 14

Approaching Rosebud Cabin

Secret Service agents Lee Wilkins and Maggie Chen had argued long and loudly against POTUS Martin Harwood and his wife abandoning their Alpine Lodge shelter. Both had been overruled decisively, the presidential parents standing firm on their decision that they would not leave their children, grandchild and daughter-in-law at the mercy of killers whose number and motives remained unknown.

Accordingly, surrounded by surviving members of federal security detail, the Harwoods trudged through snowy woods at that bleak hour of the morning, trudging first toward Rosebud Cabin, where their son, his wife and daughter Tina were presumably sequestered under guard. From there, God willing, they'd proceed to seek their daughters, hiding out from armed intruders inside Laurel Lodge.

Under prevailing Secret Service guidelines, Agents Chen

and Wilkins had authority to overrule their charges where survival was concerned. In fact, however, they had failed to make a dent in the resolve of President Harwood or First Lady Pavlina with regard to safety of their offspring.

Bottom line: Without communication between buildings at Camp David, jammed by killers who had stormed the compound, neither Chen nor Wilkins could convince the Harwoods that their loved ones were in fact secure—and neither agent chose dismissal from the Secret Service for defying their employers.

As they led the way through fading moonlight, Wilkins muttered to his female partner, "If this thing goes south on us, you know we're in the shit, right?"

Nodding in agreement, her breath pluming like the frost emitted from a deep freeze on a summer's afternoon, Chen said, "You're telling me? My money says that ship's already sailed."

"We need to make damned sure it doesn't *sink*," Wilkins advised. "Or if it does, we go down with it."

Chen cut a glance in Lee's direction. Said, "You plan on starting a late-life career, I wouldn't recommend motivational speaking."

"I'll just shut up, then, shall I?"

"Sounds like your best choice overall."

At that point, both agents stopped dead on the hiking trail they had been following, their weapons raised and pointing off into the woods ahead.

"You heard that, too?" Wilkins inquired.

"Damn straight. Somebody coming this way."

"More than one?"

"Sounded like two, at least," Chen said.

Edging a yard apart, both agents waited for a target to appear before them. When that didn't happen, Wilkins shouted to the night, "That's far enough! Drop any weapons where you stand, then come on slowly. Let us see your empty hands!"

A woman's voice both agents recognized came back to them. "Try not to shoot us, will you, Agent Wilkins?"

Maggie Chen replied to that. "Sara? Sara Durell?"

"Plus one," the disembodied CIA officer's voice replied.

"And I'm the plus one," said a man they couldn't see yet, but his voice roused other recent memories.

President Harwood answered that himself. "Colonel McConnell?"

"In the flesh, sir, more or less," the president's Marine Corps pilot answered back.

"Come on ahead, then," Harwood said, ignoring anxious looks from Agents Chen and Wilkins.

Sara answered for them both. "Coming ahead, sir."

Both new arrivals on the scene approached the presidential party cautiously. Sara was carrying an automatic rifle, while McConnell had a pistol tucked into his belt. Both looked bedraggled, weary from the hardships they'd survived so far tonight.

"It's good to see you both," Pavlina Harwood said.

"Sorry about the circumstances, ma'am," Sara replied.

McConnell chimed in next, telling the president, "If you're

all headed for the heliport, I have to tell you it's a waste of time. The chopper's wrecked and it will be a while before any relief can land."

"Grim tidings," Martin Harwood said, "but first we need to find our children. Rosebud Cabin first, then Laurel Lodge."

"We'll come along with you if that's all right, sir," Sara said.

"The more the merrier," their president replied, half-choking on a bitter-sounding laugh.

Lee Wilkins chimed in, asking Blades, "You're missing someone aren't you, Colonel? What about Jack Cody?"

"He isn't with us," Sara said, before McConnell had a chance to answer.

"Wait," the POTUS said. "He's not—?"

"No, sir," Sara replied. "At least, not that we know of. He's around here somewhere, doing other things."

"Such as?" the president inquired.

"Hunting," Sara replied.

"Cette merde est ridicule!" Marcel Bouchez muttered.

"You think I learned to speak French overnight?" Nino Nazzari asked.

"I said, 'This shit's ridiculous'."

"In that case, I agree with you. *Questa merda è ridicola.* It pays well, though."

"If we live long enough to spend the money," Bouchez groused.

Neither member of Nick Blair's team had argued with

their boss when he'd instructed them to leave him on his own and make for Alpine Lodge, to verify that other mercenaries has eliminated President Harwood and first lady. Jamming all communications at Camp David meant Blair could not simply use his two-way radio to check on Hans Behrens and Adriaan Coetzee, assigned to take out anyone they found at Alpine Lodge. Now, Bouchez and Nazzari were proceeding in that general direction, taking care to watch for roving Secret Service agents or U.S. Marines along the way.

"You volunteered, no?" asked Nazzari.

"I saw dollar signs," Bouchez replied. "What can I tell you, Nino?"

"But you've started to regret it, eh?"

"I made my choice, and now I have to live with it. *Ou mourir avec elle*, eh?"

"Do you expect to die with it instead?" Nazzari asked.

"*Connard!* You claim to speak no French."

"I also lie sometimes. *Cosa posso dirti?*"

"You have been holding out on— Wait! What's that?" Bouchez hissed at his comrade.

"*Che cosa?* I hear nothing."

"Listen! Those are voices, *ne sont-ils pas?*"

Nazzari held his breath and strained his ears, finally nodding. "*Sì.* And one of them sounds like a woman."

"Maybe Blair was right to send us, after all," Bouchez advised.

"One of the Harwood women, possibly," Nazzari said.

"Or else a Secret Service agent serving one of them, for

when *la cagna* needs some privacy."

"An agent would remain with whoever she's been assigned to guard," Nazzari said, thinking ahead.

"And now," Bouchez replied, smiling by moonlight, "they are coming straight to us."

✳✳✳

President Martin Harwood had been living in the public eye, under a microscope and floodlights, since he'd entered local politics and started climbing up the winding mountain trail that ultimately led him to the White House. Sometimes, those long years and all the labor he'd put into them seemed like a dream.

Tonight, his dream had turned into a waking nightmare.

Holding one of Lina's gloved hands in his own, he suddenly felt smaller than he had in years—perhaps in decades. Men he'd never met, of whom he knew nothing at all, had spent the night trying to kill him, with his wife and their extended family. From what he'd seen at Alpine Lodge, and now heard from Sara Durell, a number of those would-be murderers had sacrificed themselves in that attempt, not as deranged Muslim jihadists, but as calculating men who'd clearly planned on living through the night, only to have their luck and lives run out on them.

How many more still prowled the woodlands of Camp David, hunting him?

How had Cody fared so far, at hunting *them*?

Harwood never knew the answers to those questions, but if he intended to discover them, he had to stay alive himself, preserve his wife, their children, and as many of his allies in the compound as he could.

Ahead of Harwood and his wife, Agents Wilkins and Chen had stopped again, Lee with a fist raised in the universal sign to other members of their party, telling them to stop and bite their tongues.

"What's this now, Martin?" Lina asked him, barely whispering, her lips close to his ear.

"You know as much as I do," he replied.

Ahead of them, Lee Wilkins once again launched into his routine, commanding that the strangers drawing nearer to the presidential party stop dead and identify themselves.

Another voice that Harwood recognized came from the darkness. "DCI James Corbett," it proclaimed.

And in the wake of those words, one more well-known voice. "And Whit Jones, White House chief of staff."

Both men came forward slowly, cautiously, at a command from Wilson. Jones winced as he a saw the guns confronting him. Jim Corbett drew the left side of his coat back to reveal a pistol tucked into his waistband. Whit Jones followed his example, clearly trembling.

"We got these from Dogwood Cabin," Corbett said. "Fighting our way out past the man who killed our Secret Service detail."

"One man did that?" Lee Wilkerson demanded.

"And he would've done the same to us," Corbett replied,

"except we caught a break."

"One less to deal with later," said the president. "We all could use some good news about now."

Jones asked where they were going, and his boss explained their mission to retrieve the other members of his family, adding, "I hope you'll both come with us."

Whit's nod was a little jerky, taut nerves working at cross purposes to his relief.

Corbett stiffened his back and squared his shoulders, answering, "We're with you, Mister President."

Sara Durell got the last word in, telling them, "And if we're going, we should get a move on. Every minute wasted now makes targets of us all."

⁂

"*Ils arrivent*," Marcel Bouchez whispered.

"English, *dannazione!*" Nino Nazzari hissed back at him.

"They're coming, *bête*."

The two mercenaries crouched on either side of what they took to be a hiking path, since deer and other wildlife of that size could not pass through Camp David's fences to create game trails. Both men were armed with Mark 18 CQBRs and M203 grenade launchers, though their sidearms differed. Bouchez packed an H&K USP9, Nazzari favoring a Glock 19.

"Grenades first, eh?" Nazzari asked.

"Better the carbines," Bouchez answered. "Otherwise, how will the bodies be identified?"

Nino considered that, then nodded. Marcel heard the former COMSUBIN member depress his rifle's safety to the "OFF" position.

Click!

How loud it sounded to the Frenchman, with their enemies approaching, some of them conversing cautiously, their voices low-pitched. Bouchez wished that he could see them, count heads and decide how best to strafe their group for maximum effect.

The calculations came as second nature to him. Firing on fully automatic, at 950 rounds per minute, the twin carbines would expend their thirty-round box magazines in less than three seconds. Short bursts would make their ammunition last longer, but it would also risk allowing some of their intended targets to leap off the hiking path and under cover.

Bouchez had yet to see how many people were approaching their ambush. If Secret Service agents guarded others in the group—a certainty in Marcel's mind, what Nick Blair might have called a "lead-pipe cinch"—he could expect those guards to carry pistols, some of them with shotguns, submachine guns, maybe automatic rifles. All would be well-trained, but he supposed that few of them, perhaps none, would have shot a man before tonight, much less a skilled and well-armed enemy.

Attacks on U.S. heads of state made news around the world, and no such incidents had been reported since mid-June 2016. In that case, when a twenty-year-old British mental patient brought a pistol to a presidential campaign rally in

Nevada, no shots had been fired. The bumbling gunman was arrested without incident, pled guilty on reduced charges and spent five months in prison, after which he was deported to his homeland for confinement to a psychiatric ward.

In fact, to Marcel's certain knowledge, prior to this night, no U.S. Secret Service agent had used deadly force against a would-be presidential murderer since 1950, when two Puerto Rican nationalists tried to assassinate Harry Truman, killing a D.C. policeman instead.

The ambush would not be a "piece of cake", as some Americans might say, Bouchez thought he and Nazzari had an edge over their enemies.

In which case, why did Marcel feel a tremor in his hands?

***

Owen McConnell put no stock in "psychic mediums", but there had been occasions in his life when something—call it intuition or a gut instinct—had saved him from a situation where he might well have been killed. It happened frequently to soldiers fighting for their lives in combat zones, and likewise to police, firefighters and the like, from what he understood.

Blades had one of those feelings now, nothing that he could put his finger on, but an uneasiness that slowed his footsteps, made him more alert to his surroundings than if he were simply strolling through Camp David to relax.

Instinctively, he reached inside his coat pocket and drew

the SIG Sauer P229 pistol Sara Durell had loaned to him after they met while she was on her way to check the compound's helipad.

Beside him, Sara caught his movement, leaning in to ask him quietly, "What is it, Blades?"

"Nothing, I hope," he said. "I've got a creepy feeling, though."

Instead of questioning his judgment, Sara eased the safety on her SR-16 carbine to its setting for successive three-round bursts and eyed the trees surrounding them more closely, seeking anything that didn't seem to fit as part of the landscape.

A moment later, Owen said, "It might be nothing. This has been a weird damned night."

"You'll get no argument from me on that score," Sara said.

"I may be getting too old for this shit," McConnell said.

"Don't count yourself out yet, Owen."

A Secret Service agent walking to McConnell's left— Blades hadn't caught his name and figured that it didn't matter anyway—leaned in and asked, "Is something wrong, Colonel?"

"I doubt it," Blades replied. "Just getting jumpy in my old age."

"On a night like this," the agent answered, "jumpy is the only way to be."

Before McConnell could reply to that, the agent seemed to stumble, lurched against him, eyes wide and his mouth agape, vomiting blood all down the front of Owen's coat.

And a split-second after that, the whole thing went to Hell, with automatic weapons firing at them in the misty darkness, bullets buzzing in a crisscross pattern, some ripping through flesh while others came to rest in tree trunks or zipped off into the endless night.

Owen hit the deck, heard Sara land beside him and a few feet to his right, while Secret Service agents walking point began unloading with their SMGs, carbines and shotguns. They were making noise, doing their best to neutralize the ambush, but as far as Blades could tell, they weren't making a difference.

Not yet, at least.

And in a few more moments, they might all be dead.

✱✱✱

Sara Durell wanted to fire her automatic carbine, cut the opposition down or drive them back, but at the moment she was stymied. All the people she could see were members of the presidential party, while her enemies were cloaked in darkness, nothing but their muzzle flashes visible.

And if she opened up on them, she would be firing *through* her allies, blowing them away.

Beside Sara and to her left, Owen McConnell got a shot off from his SIG P229, the loud *bang* of its .357 round stinging her eardrums. She couldn't tell if he'd hit anything, but she had only seen two weapons ripping into them from ambush, both still firing after Blades squeezed off his Magnum round.

If she could only get a clear shot...

But the answer to that problem wasn't waiting for the president, his wife, or anybody else to clear her line of fire. If none of them felt free to move aside, that *she* would have to move instead.

That sounded difficult, with bullets hissing just above her head, but Sara found that she could pull it off by rolling to her right, away from Blades McConnell, drawing closer to the forest trail's north side. From that perspective, she lost track of one shooter—or maybe he'd stopped firing for the moment, trying to reload—but Sara found she had a better angle on the nearer of their adversaries.

Better, but not great.

In front of her, she saw one of the party's Secret Service agents—Lee Wilkins, she thought it must be—drop onto the trail, one big hand clutching at his throat. Blood spouted from between his fingers, telling Sara that a slug had torn through his carotid artery.

Call that a guaranteed kill shot, unless a trauma team was standing by to patch him up, and in their present situation Sara couldn't even offer him a Band-Aid. That gave her a hopeless feeling, but she turned the morbid grief around, recycled it as rage, and framed the enemy's next muzzle in her carbine's Vortex Optics Strikefire 2 Red-Green Dot Sight.

She held that picture for a fraction of a second, then squeezed off a single 5.56mm NATO round, most of her weapon's recoil operating to eject the spent shell case and feed a fresh cartridge into the SR-16's chamber.

Down range, Sara saw the hostile shooter's weapon jerk

and wobble, spitting flame and sudden death off target, then rebound to find their path again, angling for anyone and everyone who lay exposed.

Sara fired a second shot and heard a yelp of pain, some words she couldn't translate in her head.

Why would one of the snipers bent on killing them be speaking French?

"Putain de merde!"

Marcel Bouchez regretted crying out, even as he was doing so, but it was too late. Spoken words could never be recalled, only lamented at leisure.

Assuming he survived.

One rifle bullet had come close enough to spoil his aim, although it missed him, and he'd been recovering a second later, when a second slug tore through his left armpit. Doctors would call that the axilla, one of many anatomical descriptions fighting men must memorize in order to defeat, maim, or to kill their enemies.

The armpit is a delicate location on the human body, rife with nerves and lymph nodes, each concealing an axillary vein, axillary artery, and their smaller branches. Thrusting a hand under his camo jacket, Bouchez drew back fingers streaked with blood, but not enough to indicate a lethal or disabling wound. The pain was serious, but overall, Bouchez thought he had mainly suffered trauma to some muscle— probably the teres minor and/or pectoralis major that would hamper arm movement until they healed.

Again, if he was fortunate to live that long.

Grinding his teeth against the fierce pain, Bouchez raised his CQBR rifle, angling toward the figures on the hikers who had mostly scattered now, going to ground or ducking behind trees for shelter. On the far side of the trail, Nino Nazzari hissed at him, "Are you all right, *mio amico!*"

"*Bien,*" Marcel replied, before remembering to translate. "Fine." Stage-whispering, he told Nino, "I'm switching to grenades."

It did not matter now, he thought, if those he meant to kill could overhear him. Where could they escape to in the next few moments, without running back along the path in plain view of two riflemen?

Besides, grenades were less discriminating than gunfire, and Bouchez pitched with his right arm, unhampered by a painful injury.

Before the ambush, he had argued against using hand grenades for fear the bodies left behind would prove unrecognizable. Now that one of the *enculés* had wounded him, Marcel no longer cared.

As long as none of those escaped, it made no difference.

The media would trumpet who had died here in the battle for Camp David, and Blair's sponsors would be satisfied.

Bouchez would bank his final payment as agreed and find a tropic beach where no one knew his name or gave a damn, as long as he had cash in hand.

For now, though, a grenade was in his right hand, and it

cost Marcel another jolt of pain to yank its pin free with his left. He bit his tongue, refrained from crying out again, and braced himself on one knee, drawing back his arm to make the toss.

Down range, in front of him, the targets who were still alive kept firing randomly into the forest, unable to stand and get a decent fix on Nino's spitting carbine while his bullets forced their heads down into snow and muck.

Marcel was on the verge of tossing his grenade when something struck his chest, pain searing through his skin, through muscle, through his breastbone. Suddenly aware that he was pitching over backwards, he still tried to pitch the frag grenade beyond its killing range, but no part of his body was responding now.

Bouchez dropped on his back and barely felt the hand grenade land on his stomach. Glancing down at it, he almost laughed aloud, but settled for one final curse before his world dissolved into a blaze of white and red.

✳✳✳

Marine Corps Colonel "Blades" McConnell fired another .357 SIG round from his P229 semiauto, knowing it was likely wasted on the snowy night surrounding him and his companions.

That was one reason he'd volunteered for flight training when he joined the Corps, piling six hundred hours of instruction on top of mandatory graduation from the Officer

Training Corps as a commissioned second lieutenant. Today, of course, with pilots at a premium, the Corps offered pre-qualified recruits some $200,000 in bonuses that hadn't been available when Blades signed on.

Aside from childhood dreams of soaring, he'd gone through all that to serve his homeland while avoiding filthy grunt work of the kind that he was doing now.

Where had it gotten him? Prone in the snow, slush soaking through his clothes, while faceless strangers tried to kill him, just for being in the wrong place at the wrong damned time.

If he was going to survive this hellish night, McConnell knew that he must up his game and think outside the cockpit of a helicopter gunship or a fixed-wing warplane. He was in the shit now, fighting for his life like any other combat leatherneck throughout the Corps' 245 years of blood-drenched history.

And he would have to do it soon.

McConnell had a plan, in fact, although it didn't please him. Estimating odds, he pegged them in the neighborhood of nine to one that he would wind up dead or hit badly enough that he was bound to die before Camp David was relieved.

But if he pulled it off...

McConnell didn't try to share his plan with anybody else, much less Sara Durell, who had her hands full fighting for her own life and would only try to talk him out of it. Instead, he started crawling to his left, trusting the noise of other guns to cover any dragging, scraping sounds he made while slithering through snow.

When he was off the hiking path, no hostiles aiming automatic fire at him, McConnell shifted to the crazy part of his idea: a slow creep forward, closing on the enemy whose place was marked only by muzzle flashes in the night.

If he could move in close enough to spot the guy, take aim and put him down, Blades and the other members of his party just might have a chance of living through the night.

Not much of one, granted. But sure, a slender chance.

And if he failed, so what?

It wasn't all that far from where he lay right now to reach his final resting place, beneath white marble and the manicured cemetery grass at Arlington.

✳✳✳

Nino Nazzari dropped his empty CQBR magazine and fed a fresh one into the carbine, ducking as another burst of automatic fire ripped through low-hanging branches of a table-mountain pine that sheltered him.

Enemy fire was coming closer to Nazzari by the second, and he'd get no further help from poor Marcel Bouchez, who'd literally gone out with a bang some moments earlier. Nino had missed his partner's close-up technicolor death, but everyone within a hundred yards had heard the blast and seen the fireball that obliterated the late Frenchman.

Rest in pieces.

Now, Nazzari had to disengage from his determined enemies and make tracks for the exfiltration point that Nick Blair had selected. If the other mercs were there ahead of him, they could evacuate the compound as a fighting unit.

If he wound up there alone...well, tough luck, *amici*. Nino didn't plan on waiting for the others if delay put him at further risk.

Their sponsor still owed him a cool half-million dollars, and Nazzari planned on getting that, no matter what it took. Blair didn't frighten him, and by the time Nino was finished grilling him for their employer's I.D. and his whereabouts, Blair wouldn't frighten anybody else, ever again.

But first, Nazzari had to get his ass out of the death trap laid for others, which had backfired on him, killed Bouchez, and now threatened to do the same for Nino.

"Fanculo questa merda!" he muttered to himself and started backing out of the position in the pine tree's shadow. Just a few more yards, and he could scramble to his feet, start running for his life while his surviving adversaries wasted ammunition on the trees and undergrowth.

And Nino almost made it, scooting backward like a crab, knowing the greatest risk would come when he was forced to turn his back on active enemies and flee.

Almost.

Just as he pushed up off the snow, trying to stand, a figure lurched into his line of sight, pistol extended in a black-gloved hand. Nazzari was surprised that anyone could take him by surprise under the circumstances, creeping up unnoticed, closing within ten to fifteen feet of him.

The gunman started firing at him, striking Nino in one

shoulder, in his stomach and his chest. Acting on reflex, Nino squeezed the trigger of his CQBR carbine, milking two short bursts out of its magazine before his legs gave out and dropped him on his backside in the snow.

Dying, Nazzari had the satisfaction of seeing his killer twist, stagger and fall, one hand clasped to his neck, where dark blood spurted through the fingers of his glove. Before the moon winked out above him, Nino had the satisfaction of one final kill.

He would not enter the eternal darkness by himself.

In fact, Nazzari knew he would have lots of company.

***

"Is he…I mean…?"

"He's gone," Sara Durell replied to the first lady's halting question. "Took the second shooter with him, anyway."

At work—and more particularly, in the heat of battle—Sara kept a lid on her emotions, well aware that anger, fear, and all the rest of it betrayed an inner weakness that could get her killed.

But it was different when she stood over the remains of a good friend, her fingers still blood-slick from checking Blades McConnell for a pulse that wasn't there.

"His sacrifice won't be forgotten," Martin Harwood said.

Sara didn't doubt the president's sincerity, but what good was it now? If they survived the night, then what? Would Harwood nominate McConnell for his final decoration, perhaps a posthumous Medal of Honor for giving his life to defend the Commander in Chief?

Blades deserved it, in her view, but as for his sacrifice being remembered, Sara knew the truth on that score. Owen would become a footnote to the slaughter at Camp David, no matter who else came out of it alive. In time, he'd be forgotten by the vast majority of U.S. citizens, like all the other heroes who had gone before him, crowded ranks of them receding into history as far back as the first year of the Civil War.

Once the collective consciousness digested everything about this night that pundits in the media were privileged to share, America would move on to its next crisis, and to the next one after that. Owen McConnell would be relegated to an article on Wikipedia, the details of his life most likely garbled beyond recognition by the friends he left behind.

"I wish that we could take him with us," said the president, "but—"

"No, sir," Sara beat him to it. "There's no way. No way at all."

Along with Blades, they'd lost Lee Wilkins and another Secret Service agent Sara didn't know by name. A third was wounded but could walk without assistance—for the moment, anyway. More shots had grazed Whit Jones and Agent Maggie Chen, but otherwise their party had come through the ambush in fair shape.

Now, all they had to do was keep on moving through a free-fire zone, in search of Gary Harwood's family and his two sisters.

Simple, Sara thought, and almost laughed aloud at that before she caught herself.

It would take a minor miracle, in Sara's view, to find all members of America's first family alive and well after tonight. Hell, maybe it would be a *major* miracle, if she believed such things existed.

As to what might follow once the raiders were collected and identified, she didn't have a clue. The night's toll wouldn't rival 9/11 by a long shot, but if the assailants turned out to be agents of some foreign power, Sara could foresee a public clamoring for war.

And if some of them managed to escape? What, then?

She might well be assigned to track them down and bring them back, alive or dead.

That was the kind of job she'd normally assign to Jack Cody, a mission he would happily accept.

And speaking of Cody, exactly where in Hell was he right now?

CHAPTER 15

Jack Cody, at the moment Sara thought of him, was hunting men.

Their numbers had been whittled down since their invasion of Camp David started, but he still had no clear fix on how many were left or where they might be found. With that in mind, he worked a grid as the full moon prepared to set and cast Camp David into winter darkness once again.

Discovering his enemies would take a stroke of luck—and Cody got one as his wristwatch told him it was 3:16 a.m.

The trail was not one of the compound's normal paths for hiking or riding on horseback. Instead, it showed where a lone traveler on foot had trampled over chicory, ground ivy, mountain laurel and false hellebore, sumac and Japanese stiltgrass, blazing a track that ran from northeast to southwest, as indicated by the plants that had been trampled underfoot.

Someone, alone, was heading toward the compound's southwestern perimeter, where previous disruption of Camp

David's power source rendered the once-electrified barrier fence useless.

One man fleeing, but at present that was all Cody had.

And if his luck held out, it might be all he needed.

Either way, it was the only option open to him now.

The moon was nearly down, but starlight still reflected from snow covering the ground to light his way as Cody pursued his quarry through the night. As he proceeded, he considered all the ways his manhunt could go wrong.

One possibility, he realized, was that he might be following a Secret Service agent by mistake. Suppose one had been isolated somehow during the attack, cut off from backup and deprived of outside contact by the jammers that had turned the camp into a dead zone. How would such an agent, stripped of viable alternatives, react?

One smart way could involve escaping from the compound, doing whatever he could to rally help from Thurmont, Emmitsburg, or the Catoctin Naval Base. That meant a grueling hike, but it was preferable to remaining trapped inside Camp David's fence, waiting for infiltrators to attack and take out him or her.

If Cody chased a fed, only to find that he'd been wrong from the beginning, it would be a crucial waste of time, during which interval his enemies might nail the president, his family, or the prime minister of Israel.

Even so, at this point, it was still the only game in town.

And Cody had to play the hand he had been dealt.

***

Nick Blair had spent his whole life practicing control of his emotions, mastering a poker face that almost always hid what he was feeling, thinking, planning.

Almost always.

With the prostitutes he hired for physical relief, Blair kept his mask in place, surrendering to sweet sensation only at the climax—his; he didn't care about the hooker's—then dismissing her (or them) with cash in hand and orders to forget where they had spent the night.

He sometimes feigned enjoyment on appropriate occasions, such as closing a fat contract for his services with someone who required elimination of a given target, be that mark an individual, a group of persons, or—on multiple occasions, like tonight—a village, an encampment or a settlement—that his employer of the moment wanted to eradicate.

But only in his solitary moments did he vent frustration, indecision, even fear—and only in a carefully controlled setting where no clues would be left behind. Since sixth or seventh grade, the only time a living soul had seen behind his eyes occurred when Blair's rage was unleashed in mortal combat.

Now, as Blair retreated from Camp David and the mission he regarded as a failure, no concealed observer could have read his mood. He moved with purpose, walked a straight line through the snowy woods, intent upon a destination which only a mind-reader could have divined.

And mind-readers, in Blair's experience, did not exist outside of fantasy, where you might find them gamboling across Elysian Fields with unicorns and the Abominable Snowman.

Blair was pulling out, leaving his men behind, forsaking hope of final payment for the task commissioned by Thad Resnikoff. His team had managed to invade Camp David as requested, and made mincemeat of the compound's military guards, but as to their preeminent objective—taking out the U.S. President and the prime minister of Israel—well, Blair had no reason to believe that they had even earned the arms dealer's exorbitant payment.

The new day's headlines might prove otherwise, at least to some extent. Blair thought there was an outside possibility his troops had managed to eliminate some members of the presidential family, perhaps his children, maybe even his granddaughter, but that was irrelevant in terms of honoring his contract.

All Blair could say, right now, was that in his own estimation he had failed.

Of course, there would be no refund for Resnikoff. If Blair's employer wanted to hire other mercenaries for a grudge match, chasing Blair around the globe, the tattooed warrior was prepared to make them pay for that vendetta with their lives.

And if they did manage to corner him—an outcome Blair had long accepted as the likely finish of his life—he would meet death as he had doled it out to countless others in his time, refusing to let anyone observe a hint of weakness, much less fear.

Blair's destination was Camp David's southwestern perimeter, where he would cut the fence with no fear of high voltage frying him alive and slip into the night. Another two miles overland, and he would reach the Polaris Ranger all-terrain vehicle he had stashed and camouflaged ahead of time, fleeing the scene of his embarrassment and vanishing into a new identity.

Another life.

Beyond that, whatever was meant to happen *would* happen, with no assistance from Nick Blair in terms of panic, muddle-headed haste, or—

What was that?

Blair paused, immobile, with his boots planted in snow. He listened to the night, waiting for any repetition of the sound that had arrested his progress, setting his nerves on edge.

Of course, he knew there were a thousand reasons for a twig to snap—disturbance by a forest animal, surrender to the weight of snow or ice, even an errant breeze. It was not necessarily a human footstep, and it clearly didn't mean someone was tracking Blair, seeking to take him down.

Not necessarily.

But Nick Blair had to know for sure, beyond the shadow of a doubt.

To simply shrug it off could be madness. Worse, it struck him as incompetence.

And that was one thing Blair could not abide.

Secret Service agent Maggie Chen had taken point to lead the presidential party—what was left of it—toward Camp David's main gate. Their dogged footsteps squeaked and crunched on frozen snow, as if the group's members were walking over Styrofoam.

She guessed that from an aerial perspective, they must look like extras from *The Walking Dead*.

Except, of course, this wasn't Hollywood or a sound stage in Georgia, and tonight's dead were not walking.

They'd been left behind to chill out literally, in the frosty woods.

Although she'd seen him die, Chen still couldn't entirely grasp the fact that Lee Wilkins was gone for good. She'd never look into his eyes again or feel his soft touch as his fingers brushed a stray lock of her hair back from Chen's face. They'd never—

Stop it, damn you!

She and Wilkins had concealed their after-hours hookups from their various superiors, no small achievement, given that the Secret Service was a hyper-vigilant outfit, attached since 2003 to the U.S. Department of Homeland Security. They lived under a microscope, complete with random polygraphs and drug tests, making their shared secret all the more remarkable.

Not that it mattered now.

Maggie was grief-stricken, but otherwise could not have said exactly how she felt about Lee being slain before her very eyes. They'd also lost another agent—Harry Claiborne—in the recent firefight, plus the president's Marine Corps pilot, Colonel Owen "Blades" McConnell, but if Agent Chen had claimed their deaths affected her the same way Lee's had, she would have been lying.

If there was an upside to the skirmish, it was taking out two of the terrorists who'd laid siege to Camp David. Sadly, neither one of them had been gunned down by Secret Service agents, but whoever put them down—Sara Durell and Blades McConnell, almost with his dying breath—Maggie was satisfied that two assholes were out of action, while the treasury could dodge spending a fortune on their trials.

Now, if she could only get the dazed survivors of the Harwood party to a safe place, without snipers lurking in the forest, Maggie would be satisfied. Her long day would drag on, of course, being debriefed, typing and signing her report in triplicate, but sometime in the day ahead she would be free to shower, change her clothes, and have a glass of wine or three.

Thinking about the world outside reminded Chen to check her walkie-talkie. She expected nothing from it, figured that her enemies would still be jamming frequencies across the board, but still, it couldn't hurt to try.

And this time, when she got an answer—faint and staticky at first, then clear and strong—she nearly dropped her radio before she said, "Wait one," and turned to face the president.

A dozen faces gaped at her, as she announced, "We have contact!"

***

Cody mouthed a silent curse and stopped dead in his tracks.

Too late.

He couldn't jump into a nonexistent time machine, go back and stop a twig from snapping when he stepped on it. There was a chance his quarry might have missed the sound, or else ignored it, but assuming that to be the case was a shortcut to oblivion.

And not at all the way that "Suicide" Cody hoped to die.

After a full minute that felt more like an hour, he allowed himself to move again, more slowly, cautiously along the path he had been following for roughly half a mile now. Every one of Cody's senses was on high alert—eyes, ears, his nostrils seeking out a human's scent, even breathing through his mouth as if to taste the chilly forest air.

And he was almost certain that his human prey *had* registered the faint sound, was reacting to it by a hasty effort to devise an ambush on the trail.

But *almost certain* wasn't damned sure good enough.

Immediately, Cody knew that he had four options.

First, he could remain frozen in place, waiting to hear if his quarry began to move again, but that might take all night.

Second, he could proceed along the trail with greater caution, hoping that no hastily devised trap lay in wait for him.

Third, he could veer off-course and try to parallel the fugitive's escape route without making any more unnecessary noise, hoping to intercept his target closer to the camp's fence line.

Or fourth, he could do something crazy, call attention to

himself and force his adversary's hand.

One way of doing that was verbally. He could call out into the darkness, warn his enemy deliberately, hoping that the unseen individual would answer back, either in words or with a burst of gunfire that would let Cody peg his whereabouts.

The other way, since he possessed no hand grenades, would be to strafe the forest with his CQBR carbine, probing bursts to rout his target or—with any luck at all—wound him.

A quick kill wasn't what he had in mind, though.

He was after information, anything to tell him why armed men had stormed the presidential compound and at whose behest.

But failing that, his target—unlike others he'd picked off so far tonight—might have some I.D. on his person, or instructions on a cell phone that could be traced to their source.

From there…

Jack stopped himself from speculating any further, traipsing down a road of wishful thinking that might just as easily bring him up short, at a dead end.

He cast his silent vote—the only one that mattered now—for what he'd call Option 4A.

Crouching behind the stout bole of a venerable sugar maple tree, he shouted up the trail, "You're done, pal. This is your one and only chance to stay alive."

The mercenary must have doubted Jack, responding with a burst of automatic fire that flayed bark from the sugar maple's trunk and clipped a couple of its lower-hanging limbs.

***

"Stupid bastard!" Nick Blair cursed under his breath.

Meaning himself, that was, for letting anybody get this close to him while he was just a couple hundred yards from slicing through Camp David's fence and getting clean away. If he'd been more alert, more cautious, more *something,* he would have cleared the property within a few more minutes and been well along toward his escape.

"Dumb shit!" he hissed, aware that anytime he cursed himself, his voice inevitably sounded like his alcoholic father's, if that prick had still been drawing breath.

He hadn't been Blair's first kill, but his death still ranked among the mercenary leader's top five memories.

In fact, he viewed it as a service to mankind, shutting the douchebag's mouth for good.

Snap out of it, a small voice in his head commanded.

That one sounded like his own.

Better.

Blair fired off a full half-magazine from his Mark 18 CQBR, confident that he hadn't drawn blood, preferring gunfire over chit-chat when he couldn't guarantee his voice would be as firm and steady as he liked. When no one sent a storm of bullets flying back his way, Blair thumbed an M576 buckshot canister into his M203 40mm launcher and sent its score of 1.9-gram metal pellets ratcheting down range.

He paused and waited then, hoping for moans or cries of pain that would denote a wounded enemy, although he couldn't trust his unknown foe to play it straight. If their positions were reversed, Blair would have faked an injury, pleading for mercy, anything at all to bring his adversary within striking range.

And what he got was…nothing.

Silence is a weapon, in and of itself. How many so-called loving couples had been torn apart by failure to communicate? Millions, at least.

How many parents had been lulled into an apathy that verged on catalepsy by their silent children who were still too young for slasher films or coffee, much less sex and drugs?

In court, silence could not be treated as acceptance of an offer, and would sink a frivolous lawsuit, while an amnesiac eyewitness could release a psycho killer to inflate his body count.

When he'd reloaded his grenade launcher—an M356 HE round this time, meant to detonate on impact with the ground or other solid objects, thereby setting off its booster charge and killing anyone within a radius of sixteen feet, inflicting wounds out to twenty-seven times that distance.

Blair would hold that in reserve, until he glimpsed his enemy, and in the meantime he could wait. But damn it, not for too much longer.

Common sense told Blair that he was swiftly running out of time.

***

Jack Cody counted off ten seconds silently, then eased off to the left or southwest of the sugar maple tree that had absorbed FMJ slugs and buckshot meant for him. He moved slowly, taking extraordinary care to plant his feet without making another telltale sound.

The frozen snow was treacherous, a natural noisemaker, he managed half a dozen decent strides without crunching or creaking to betray his plan.

Arriving at the spot he'd chosen, in the shadow of a black birch tree that stood some sixty feet in height. Peering around it, Cody scanned the path he'd left behind, eyes narrowed, wishing he had goggles to protect them from the cold, watching for any hint of movement, any shape or shadow that stood out as alien and therefor dangerous.

He spent at least four minutes staring, listening for any sound, before he found what he was seeking. Fifty feet or so in front of him, a patch of darkness shifted slightly to his left, the faceless watcher's right, playing the same game Cody had initiated with his move off course.

Were sharp eyes that he couldn't see watching him raise his SR-16 carbine, snug its butt plate to his shoulder, index finger curling gently to enfold its trigger?

If he had been spotted, Cody's adversary gave no sign of it.

Five seconds more elapsed.

Cody acquired his target with the carbine's flip-up sight, released his pent-up breath, then sent a three-round burst of boat-tail FMJ rounds sizzling down range at thirty-one hundred feet per second. Impact produced a loud, wet round immediately followed by a stifled cry and tumbled out into the open, sprawling on the snow.

He lunged forward instantly, closing the gap between him and his fallen enemy, suspecting that the wounded man still had some fight left in him and would try to take advantage of Cody's rush. Before the downed man could return fire, Cody triggered a single round that tore into the stranger's right shoulder, wrenching another cry out of him, spinning his assault rifle away and beyond reach.

"That's it," Cody announced. "But if you want to try the Desert Eagle on your hip, feel free. My next round takes your elbow on that side."

The voice that answered him was strained and croaking, how Cody thought a man-sized frog might sound. "No, thanks. Feels like I'm dying as it is."

"You must have figured that was possible," Cody said. "I mean, before you took the job."

"Nobody lives forever, right?"

"No one I ever heard of, anyway."

"So, is this where you tell me I still have a chance? Answer a few quick questions and you'll whisk me off to supermax?"

"You've got me mixed up with a DA or a judge," Cody replied.

"But you still want information, right? You would have put me down already, otherwise."

"You *are* down," Cody reminded him. "Just not out, yet."

"I have to tell you, your negotiation sucks."

"I've heard it said before."

"But you still go ahead with it."

"You and your buddies killed some decent folks tonight. I tried to think of any reason you should get an easy out and came up empty."

"Easy out, you say?" The chalky voice was close to taunting now. "Is that what some fool calls a gurney and a needle at ADX Florence?"

Meaning death row for condemned federal inmates, located in Colorado.

"Just between us," Cody said, "I don't see this case winding up in court."

✳✳✳

That was the bottom line, Nick Blair decided. If he couldn't somehow kill the rifleman standing in front of him, then stanch the bleeding from his wounds, he wasn't going anywhere tonight except the nearest morgue.

"With that in mind," he said, "it's hard to see how talking to you does jack shit for me."

"There's dead," his captor answered back, "and then there's dead. I'm guessing you're conversant with the difference."

"You ever hear Tom Petty's song 'Scare Easy', hotshot?" Blair inquired.

"Skip the Top Forty reviews," his enemy replied. "Some easy answers and you drift away. Stonewall me, and we'll have to go another way."

"Such as?"

Blair had no time to flinch between the gunshot and his left kneecap disintegrating. The resultant agony, immediate and fierce, produce a shrill cry from his raspy throat.

"My bad," the shooter said. "Hair trigger. Sorry about that."

"You rotten mother—"

Bam!

This time it was his right knee, blasted into pulp that stained his winter camo trousers.

"Jesus Christ!"

His foe glanced left, then right, and shrugged. "Sorry," he said. "Nobody here but you and me."

"How long...you plan...to keep this up?" Blair stammered through his pain.

"You'll know when I run out of ammo," said his tormentor. "Then, I may have to build a fire. That's good for cauterizing wounds."

Blair was thinking that he ought to try the Desert Eagle, force this prick to finish him, but what would stop him moving on to shoulders, elbows, maybe downtown to the family jewels? Facing the guy, Blair recognized a twinge of fear beneath his pain.

The rifleman reminded Blair a good deal of himself.

Bad news, that was. A man without compunction might do anything.

"All right, dipshit," he said at last. "What do you want to know?"

"The usual. Who set this up and why? Where I can find the puppeteers?"

"As for the who, I only know one name: Thaddeus Resnikoff. You ever heard of him?"

"It rings a bell. A Russian father, British mother. One of the top arms dealers around."

"That's on the surface," Blair corrected him. "He also does his share of contracting, and I don't mean construction work."

"And he makes more from that than stocking armies with materiel?"

"A job like this, with heavy sponsors, he might clear as much for one night's work as sending tanks and helicopters halfway round the world. On certain hits, I think he might even donate his time."

"Someone he holds a special grudge against."

"It wouldn't have to be a personal insult," Blair said. "Thad's a good hater, even if he isn't banking millions for a given job."

"Okay. Just one more question."

"Let me guess. You want to know where you can find him?"

A bleak smile answered him, the gunman saying, "Funny you should ask."

✳✳✳

Cody was moving toward the fence line when the walkie-talkie on his belt hissed static for a few seconds, before white noise resolved itself into a woman's voice. As usual with such devices, quality was dubious, the voice tinny and far-away sounding, but Cody recognized it anyway.

"Sara?" he answered back. "I'd given up on reaching you."

"Same here," she said, "but something must have taken out the jammer."

"Finally. Where are you, Sara? Anybody with you?"

"Damn near everybody," she replied. "We've got all of the Harwoods back together, the prime minister, Corbett and Jones, with Secret Service agents covering."

Jack noted one omission from the list she's just recited. "Any sign of Blades?"

A fleeting hesitation, then she said, "He didn't make it, Jack."

Well, shit, thought Cody. But he said, "Okay. I'm sorry, Sara."

"Yeah, me too. Where are you, Jack?"

"I've got a line on who's behind this, thinking we should have a little chat."

"Jack…"

Before the lecture could begin, he interrupted her, asking, "Have you made contact with the outside yet?"

"Affirmative. The White House, Langley, Secret Service headquarters, the Thurmont naval base. We should be over-run with reinforcements any time now. Jack—"

"I ran into the strike team's leader, Sara. Guy named Nick Blair. Ever heard of him?"

"It doesn't ring a bell. I'll get it on the air, asap."

"No hurry, looking for him. You can find him near the southwestern perimeter, a quarter-mile or so in from the fence."

"From that, I guess he won't be giving any statements to

the feds?"

"Lucky for me, I heard his dying declaration."

"And you say he named the guy behind all this?"

"More like the middleman," Cody said. "If I can get to him before he's in the wind, I may have more names for you."

"Listen, Jack—"

He knew she was about to ask for details, tell him that a flying squad from Langley of the FBI Academy could reach the target faster that he could, smother the money man with agents and detain him without counsel under terms of the USA PATRIOT Act, but Cody wasn't listening.

By now, over the nineteen years since 9/11, most Americans had more or less forgotten the USA PATRIOT Act, passed overwhelmingly by Congress in the latter days of 2001. Fewer still could have told you that the statute's name was an acronym for a mouthful of legalese verbiage: "*U*niting and *S*trengthening *A*merica by *P*roviding *A*ppropriate *T*ools *R*equired to *I*ntercept and *O*bstruct *T*errorism Act of 2001."

Aside from reshuffling federal law enforcement organizations, the law enhanced domestic and foreign surveillance, strengthened border security, tightened money-laundering restrictions, redefined "terrorism" with stricter penalties, and effectively stripped individuals tagged as "foreign combatants" of their rights to legal counsel and a public trial.

All that, and there was still no mention in the hefty document of anything resembling Cody's one-man war.

Some things were better left unspoken, trusting—or presuming—that the vast majority of We the People didn't want to know what government was doing in their names.

"Jack?" Sara's anxious voice came back at him. "Are you still there?"

"I am," he said, "but not for long."

"You need to think this through," she said.

"Been there, done that. It's all good, Sara."

"No, it's not! At least, for God's sake, tell me where you're going? If it goes south on you—"

"Never fear. I'll text you the location when I get there."

"Jack…"

"Over and out," he said, and cut the link between them as he reached Camp David's looming fence with coils of razor wire on top.

CHAPTER 16

Baltimore/Washington International Thurgood Marshal Airport

Even its loudest boosters will admit—if only over cocktails and in private—that the full name of Baltimore's airport is awkward, not something that rolls off the tongue easily. Opened in 1950 as Friendship International Airport, built on land purchased by Uncle Sam from the Friendship Methodist Church, it only saw the name of America's first black Supreme Court justice, a Baltimore native, tacked on in 2005.

Today, most of the airport's twenty-odd million travelers yearly drop "Thurgood Marshal" from the airport's name without intending any disrespect or giving it a second thought. Air traffic controllers and pilots serving the airport's twenty-three airlines know it simply as "BWI."

Thaddeus Resnikoff was happily oblivious to the airport's history and etymology. The only thing he gave a damn about was lifting off on time and clearing U.S. air space before someone tried to slap a warrant on his ass.

Last night had disappointed him enough and cost him millions he could not afford to lose, without the added headache of arrest, followed by trial behind closed doors of a United States Foreign Intelligence Surveillance Court—"FISA" for short, in legalese.

Should that occur, with his conviction on a lengthy list of felonies inevitable, Thad Resnikoff would end his life at ADX Florence, caged with a rogue's gallery of foreign and domestic terrorists, traitorous double agents, and decrepit ex-leaders of organized crime. In supermax, a life term meant precisely that, spending twenty-three hours per day in a single, soundproof cell constructed out of poured concrete.

And that would be the *good* news.

Federal death sentences dragged on for years with various appeals, but relatively few were overturned—and if they were, so what? Even with commutation to a life term, in a system that had banned parole for any crimes committed after 1987, lucky "winners" were allowed to rot in peace until their old age, or some wasting disease released them to a crematorium.

No thank you, very goddamned much.

"Where are we going first?" Thad's passenger inquired.

"Havana," Resnikoff replied. "From there, Bermuda, then the Azores, on to Portugal, and after that, pick any place on Earth."

"We'll need to think about the extradition treaties," his companion noted, in a worried-sounding voice. As well he might.

"And you're in luck. Worldwide, seventy-three out of one hundred ninety-six nations won't return a fugitive stateside. That's more than one-third of the total, ranging from Afghanistan to Yemen alphabetically."

"Thirty-seven percent," Thad's companion corrected him. Always nit-picking.

"Just Google them," said Resnikoff, hoping to shut him up, but no such luck.

"What do you mean about me picking where to go? You plan on splitting up?"

"It's common sense," Thad said. "You've heard the saying, 'He who travels fastest goes alone'?"

"That's Kipling, right?"

"He got it from an old African proverb," Resnikoff answered.

"Why can't we stick together? I mean, for a little while, at least?"

"There's a fair chance that the FBI will have my name before long. Several countries owe me favors, not to mention cash, and will agree to shelter me. You, on the other hand, will turn up missing from your job tomorrow morning, triggering alarms as word of last night's operation spreads. The very worst thing we could do is run in tandem, leaving twice as many tracks."

"But if we can't be extradited to the States—"

"That doesn't mean we can't be *found*," Thad said, his patience feeling strained. "Remember Julian Assange?"

"Sure, from Wikileaks. But—"

Thad pressed on, talking over his associate. "Assange spent seven years holed up at the Ecuadorian embassy in London, afraid to show his face outside the compound. Ecuador revoked asylum last year, as you may recall. Now he's facing a trial for sex crimes and computer hacking. Even if the rape charge is a put-up deal, he's done."

Resnikoff didn't share his other reason for preferring solitary travel. Once the failure at Camp David was revealed worldwide, determined hunters would be on his track, seeking to punish him for the expensive cockup—and to guarantee Thad wouldn't cut a deal to name his backers in bid for leniency.

"Okay, you win," his passenger responded, sulking. "Where do we split up?"

"Havana would be best," Thad said, "but I can leave you on Bermuda, or at Angra, in the Azores. Any time before the flight to Portugal."

"I hope the plane's all right, at least."

Resnikoff smiled at that. "It cost ten million dollars new," he said, "and it costs me nineteen hundred dollars an hour to fly. If that's not good enough for you, I'll buy you a commercial ticket, flying coach."

The jet was an EMB-505 Phenom 300, developed the Brazilian aerospace manufacturer Embraer. Cody knew its specs and ran through them once more on his approach.

The Phenom seats eleven persons in a pinch: a pilot and

copilot plus nine passengers, six seated in standard configuration, plus one in the cockpit and one on the jet's belted toilet. It measures fifty-two feet from nose to tail, with low-positioned, swept wings spanning fifty-three feet. Its T-tail configuration supports two rear-pylon-mounted Pratt & Whitney Canada PW535E turbofan engines, each generating 3,360 foot-pounds of thrust, for a cruising speed of 521 miles per hour. Its range, fully loaded, was 2,268 miles, at a service ceiling of 45,000 feet.

All Cody needed to gain access was a denim jumpsuit and a tag around his neck, identifying him as a BWI aircraft maintenance man. The photo on that tag was copied from his D.C. driver's license, coupled with an alias he sometimes used while traveling inside the States on errands that did not involve bloodshed.

An airstair on the jet's left-hand side grants entry to the cockpit and cabin. The latter had a slightly claustrophobic feel about it, five feet one inch wide, seventeen feet long, with ceiling headspace of four feet nine inches requiring most adults to stoop.

One pilot was aboard when Cody climbed the stairs and made his way inside. The flyboy had his nose buried in charts and barely glanced up for a nod as Cody turned back toward the cabin. Checking out the new arrival's I.D. never crossed the crewman's mind.

So far, so good.

Aside from Cody's tool belt, he was carrying a well-worn leather satchel, which presumably contained more tools, maybe an oil can and a pressure gauge. In fact, the satchel held two Glock 21 semiauto pistols chambered in .45 ACP caliber, each fitted with a Gemtech SOS-9 sound suppressor that reduced noise of gunshots to twenty-eight decibels, shown on sound charts as the level of library whispers. Each staggered box magazine—eight in the bag, in case something went wrong—held thirteen hollow point subsonic rounds.

Also nestled in the satchel, as a hedge against reluctant answers to his questions for the jet's owner, Cody had packed a leather pouch holding an icepick, steak knife, and two pairs of pliers—needle nose and slip joint.

Cody hoped the tools would not be necessary, but he knew that wouldn't ultimately be his call.

He glanced back toward the cockpit, saw the copilot still busy with his paperwork, and stepped into the Phenom's lavatory. Cody had been in larger phone booths, when those still existed, and he wondered whether any passenger had ever sat through a takeoff or landing on the toilet, with its lap strap belted tight.

It was a mental picture that he gladly pushed aside.

Jack checked his watch, wondered why Resnikoff was running late, and hoped the FBI or Secret Service hadn't picked him off at home before he had a chance to slip away. Cody preferred a little one-on-one time with the oligarch and purveyor of death who'd sewn his dragon's teeth from Southeast Asia through the Middle East, across the width of Africa and transatlantic, to the shores of South America over the past decade.

And more specifically, he wanted to get even for last night.

Jack didn't have a final body count for the Camp David siege, but Blades McConnell was a friend—or had been, anyway, to the extent that Cody granted anyone a look beyond his grief for Carol and their murdered children.

As things stood, he didn't have enough friends left to make the loss of even one a casual affair.

Jack was considering that loss when voices sounded in the Phenom's cabin, bringing Cody to his feet, a Glock in either hand.

***

"Damn! This plane is sick!"

Thaddeus Resnikoff disdained most Western slang but recognized his fellow passenger's remark as a display of admiration. "Sick", in modern parlance, had replaced "awesome" and "cool" as expletives denoting praise.

And how appropriate was that, in such a manifestly sick society?

"No stewardesses?" asked his short-term passenger.

"They're known as flight attendants nowadays," Resnikoff said, correcting him. "And no, none will be flying with us this time."

"Bummer, man."

Thad turned to face his copilot. Said, "Eric, are we still waiting for Todd?"

"No, sir," the Phenom's second in command replied. "He's in

the terminal, grabbing a few things for the trip, last-minute."

Thad felt a slow burn starting in his stomach, creeping upward through his chest.

"I gave him our departure time."

"Yes, sir. He just—"

"Go in and fetch him, will you Eric? Anyone who's not back here and buckled up for takeoff within fifteen minutes needs to find another job. No fucking severance, and you can whistle for your benefits."

"Yes, sir!"

It pleased Thad, watching as the crewman bolted from the cockpit, down the airstair and away, running as if his life depended on it.

Which, if he failed Resnikoff now, it might.

"Glad I'm not on your bad side," his companion said, forcing a smile.

"Don't be so sure," the arms dealer replied.

"Say what?"

"You had a job to do in Florida, remember?"

"Sure, but—"

Resnikoff talked over him. "In my experience, 'but' normally proceeds a lame excuse for failure or announces an impending deviation from candor."

"I'm not sure—"

"For example, one might say, 'I don't mean to offend you, but...' What follows is, almost without exception, meant in fact to give offense."

"Okay, except—"

"Another instance might involve slacker saying, 'Yes, I meant to do it, but...' At which point he or she delivers an excuse that falls short of a valid explanation."

"Look, Thad—"

"That is Mister Resnikoff, to you."

"Okay, then. Mister—"

"Before you say another word, can you imagine any explanation, summary or commentary that will make you seem less of a failure in my eyes?"

To that, Resnikoff's temporary passenger made no reply.

"We are agreed then, yes?" Resnikoff asked.

Instead of speaking, though, his young companion was caught up in staring *past* him, toward the rear of the Phenom's cabin. Frowning, Resnikoff turned and found a stranger dressed in workman's coveralls, a plastic tag hanging around his neck, too far for Resnikoff to read despite his contact lenses.

In each hand, the stranger held a Glock, immediately recognizable to Resnikoff, despite the sound suppressors mounted on each pistol's muzzle.

"Ah," said Thaddeus, trying to mask the tremor in his voice. "I see we have a stowaway."

The man he'd never seen before replied, "Think of me as a debt collector. Your tab's overdue, asshole. But thanks for bringing me a party favor, anyway."

"I don't believe that we've been introduced," said Resnikoff.

"My bad," the stranger said. "I must have left my manners in the terminal, at duty-free. My names Jack Cody. Ever heard of me?"

"I don't believe—"

"I know him," said the arms dealer's companion, sounding almost childlike now. "He's some kind soldier, name of Cody."

"Bingo!" Cody replied. "And give that little traitor a cigar."

Resnikoff cleared his throat. "If this has anything to do with Florida, I can assure you—"

"How many assurances can you shove up your ass?" Cody inquired.

"I beg your pardon!"

"Remember what the Jewish vampire said when one of his intended victims pulled a crucifix?"

"Vampire? I don't—"

"He said, 'Oy vey, it wouldn't help you, Bubby'."

And Thad was surprised when his companion cackled at that witticism, sounding on the edge of raw hysteria.

***

"I had my doubts about you in Fort Lauderdale," Cody told Mason Narmy, age twenty-five, a hot-shot data analyst at the NSA's Puzzle Palace at Fort George G. Meade, Maryland.

"Oh, yeah? And why was that?" Narmy replied, no longer laughing now.

"First off, I thought Shayna could have done better," Cody said. "You're on the scrawny side and have that acne going on, but hey, there's no accounting for taste, right?"

"Fuck you, Jackie!"

Cody barely had to stroke the trigger of his right-hand

Glock. It coughed once, nothing audible beyond the jet's interior despite its open door. Narmy collapsed onto a strip of carpeting that ran the full length of the Phenom's cabin. Mason clutched his groin with both hands, whimpering, watching blood pulse between his fingers.

Resnikoff was holding up so far, despite a flinch when Cody shot his stooge, but he was frowning now.

The shit was getting real.

Jack faced the arms dealer and said, "Your boyfriend's feeling tongue-tied. Want to brief me on your plans for Shayna Harwood, or should I go with an educated guess?"

Instead of answering him, Resnikoff asked Jack, "How did you find me here?"

"Nick Blair. He held out for a while, then saw the light and gave you up."

"That *grebanyy sukin syn*."

"Maybe you should have paid him more up front. But, then again, there's only so much pain a man can take."

Resnikoff glanced around at Mason Narmy, found him weeping, and dismissed him with a shrug.

"My question," Cody prodded. "About Shayna."

"Ah. Why not? One of my various employers wished to cause her parents—well, her father, chiefly—some embarrassment. This one—" a backwards nod toward Narmy—"was supposed to put her antics onto video, but somehow the technology defeated him. Can you imagine that? A techie from the NSA who leaves the lens cap on or some such *chush' sobach'ya*. It's pathetic, if you think about it."

"Good help's hard to find these days," Cody agreed. "So, you decided just to snatch her?"

"An embellishment, I grant you, but it could have worked. A ransom payment for the trollop's safe return, then my employer airs the videos worldwide. A win-win, I believe your people call it."

"Some might. But the boys you sent screwed that up, too. They started shooting."

"That would be *your* fault, at least according to this sorry specimen." Another nod toward Mason Narmy, sitting in a pool of blood now, whimpering but without much conviction.

"Sorry if I spoiled your setup," Cody said.

"Are you, indeed?"

"Not even close."

"In any case, you understand the disappointment of my sponsors. If there was no scandal, they decided, then the stakes must be increased. Where better than Camp David, and with the prime minister of Israel present to confuse matters. That raised my price, of course. A patron unrelated to the plot against the Harwood family chipped in a bonus for eliminating Jairus Abramson. I feel no animosity toward him myself—as we've done business in the past and might have done again someday—but there was no refusing such a price."

"The bottom line," Cody said.

"What else is there, when all is said and done?"

"I guess you'd laugh if I said, 'Honor'."

"Laugh? No. I might be confused by such naïveté in one of your experience."

"Funny old world," Cody said.

"Your meaning is...?"

"I never met you in my life before, but now I'm pleased to disappoint you."

"Ah. A patriot. How quaint. What happens now? Should we expect a SWAT team? Handcuffs? Shackles? Am I doomed to do the 'perp walk' on Fox News?"

Cody watched Mason Narmy slump sideways and shiver through his death throes.

"No SWAT team," he promised Resnikoff. I have a little something else in mind."

***

Resnikoff did not like the sound of that, but he had long since come to terms with a conviction that he would not die in bed, of some natural cause, a withered husk at eighty-five or ninety years of age.

In truth, before he let that happen, he would almost certainly have ended his own life.

Who knew the means and methods better than a man who sold death for a living?

He glanced back at Mason Narmy again and saw no signs of life remaining. The young man sprawled like a rag doll in the Embraer's aisle, his bullet wound no longer spilling blood, but only seeping through the sodden ruin of his slacks.

"I'll let you have the same deal that I gave your front man at Camp David," Cody informed him. "Information for a speedy exit."

"That's intriguing," Thaddeus replied. "I wonder, though, what will you do about my crewmen? They should be here any minute, from the terminal. Will you eliminate them, too? Are they merely collateral damage to your employers?"

Cody's smile at that question surprised him.

"Damn," he said. "Did I forget to mention that a team of FBI agents were waiting for them in the terminal?"

"You're bluffing," Resnikoff retorted, but the hollow feeling in his stomach told him he was wrong.

"They'll have to waste the night on interviews," his captor said, "and they can kiss their jobs with you goodbye. But if they come back clean for anything except flying your ass around the world, they shouldn't wind up doing any time. And who knows? They might even remember where you've been the past few months, and maybe even who you visited. I might not need your side of it at all. Tick-tock."

"It seems you have me at your mercy," Thaddeus replied.

"Bad luck for you, then," Cody told him. "I'm fresh out."

Resnikoff hesitated for a beat, then played his final card. "What if," he said, "I could provide what you want most of all? I mean, beyond the names of my employers. Would that entitle me to any leniency?"

"It sounds like you're confused," Cody advised.

"In what sense?"

"I'm not Monty Hall, and this isn't *Let's Make a Deal.*"

"Four names," said Resnikoff. "No friends of mine, but men responsible for how you live today."

"If there's a point to this—"

"Indeed, there is," the arms dealer replied. "I know who killed your wife and children."

Cody had prepared himself for anything but that. He felt as if a fist had clenches around his stomach and was squeezing it against his spine.

"You're full of shit," he said.

"Are not we all?" asked Resnikoff. "But stop and *think* now, Mister Cody. After the cockup in Fort Lauderdale, when Mason mentioned you by name, I was unable to resist investigating further. As you might surmise, I have contacts around the world in governments, the military, various intelligence consortiums."

"And now, just by coincidence, you're offering me something that the CIA and NSA couldn't discover? After they spent years researching it?"

Resnikoff shrugged and offered the vestige of a smile.

"The agencies you mention work through channels, Jack. You don't mind if I call you Jack?"

"Just spit it out."

But Resnikoff seemed bent on telling it his way, prolonging the last moments of his time on Earth. "I live *outside* those channels, Jack. I gather information from the same groups that employ you and a host of others: the GIS in Egypt, Russia's FSB and SVR, the French DGSI, Beijing's MSS, the ISI in Pakistan..."

"I get the point," Cody said.

"Of course. I could go on all night, Jack. Nations that require my services traditionally pay in cash, but they also like to keep me on their side, as they perceive it in their own small minds. It's quite remarkable. Two countries at each other's throats, while I'm supplying arms to both, and yet those mortal enemies somehow believe I favor each of them."

"So, you're a mercenary prick. Tell me something I don't already know."

"When Mason dropped your name, it seemed expedient for me to understand you, why you chose to meddle in my business."

"Kidnapping a woman isn't business," Cody informed him. "It's a crime."

"Or, when commissioned by a would-be head of state, who is to say it's not a matter of diplomacy?"

Jack raised the Glock in his right hand. "You're drifting. And your smarmy wheeze is getting on my nerves."

"Indulge me for a moment longer, if you will."

"Right. You've got sixty seconds, starting now."

"In which case, I shall summarize. As it turns out, the search was not unduly arduous. In fact, I found the information I required at Joint Base Anacostia–Bolling, in Washington, DC."

"The DIA," Cody said.

"Exactly. Your Defense Intelligence Agency discovered the identities of those responsible for planning the attack and those who pulled the triggers. In the latter case, they are, like our friend Mason here, deceased. The individual behind it, though…well, that's another story."

Jack was barely breathing when his right-hand trigger finger twitched and Resnikoff went down, one of his kneecaps shattered into pulp. His scream echoed around the jet's cabin, then warbled off into the night.

"Are you *insane?*" Resnikoff howled.

"I've heard it said," Cody replied. "The names, right now, or else I'll have to fetch my pliers from your crapper."

"Names? But there is only one!"

"Wrong answer. Start with those behind the hit on Camp David and go from there."

"But I—"

Another muted cough, this time from Cody's left-hand Glock. Another kneecap gone. More sobbing cries.

"It's funny how you all wind up in the same place," Cody said. "Nick Blair, your boyfriend over there, now you."

"If you kill me—"

"That's 'when,' not 'if'."

"All right! Enough!" Another moment wasted moaning, then the arms dealer asked Jack, "You know the RGB?"

"From North Korea. Sure."

That was the Reconnaissance General Bureau, North Korea's primary intelligence and clandestine operations group, created in 2009."

"You're saying Kim Jong-un was dumb enough—"

"No, no," Thad interrupted him. "In this case, it was one of his subordinates, an overly ambitious general named Lee Gil-su. He secretly collaborated with a Saudi prince who thinks his star might rise if Israel lost its man in charge and those above him in the pecking order were persuaded that America is weak. If Asian sponsors were available."

"His name?"

"Yousef Khalid."

"And now, the rest."

"I'm bleeding badly."

"Then you'd better hurry up," Cody advised.

"You are familiar with the PFLP-General Command?"

Jack nodded, translating the acronym to the Popular Front for Liberation of Palestine, one of the Middle East's oldest terrorist groups, dating back to the late 1960s.

"Yes," said Resnikoff. "And you have interfered with them from time to time?"

"Could be."

"They forget nothing. And they don't forgive."

"The names. Now."

"Those who carried out the action have, alas, already passed on to their heaven, *Al-Jannah*, and claimed their vestal virgins. Their commander at the time, now seemingly retired, was Salman Mardam-Bey."

Cody stepped closer to the arms dealer. Leveled both pistols at his face. "I'll check that out," he said.

"And I can help you! If you just—"

The twin Glocks coughed as one. Resnikoff's head imploded, bits and pieces of it decorating the two seats behind him.

Jack retreated to the jet's restroom, stowed his hardware

inside the satchel, took it with him as he left the plane and rattled down its airstair.

Moving toward his rented car, he palmed his cell phone, hit speed dial, and waited through two rings.

"All done?" Sara Durell inquired.

"Except for calling out the hearse."

"Do you have names for me?"

"If you can trust them," Cody replied, and passed along the information Resnikoff had shared.

"We'll check it out," Sara replied.

"There's more."

"Okay."

"What do you know about a PFLP honcho—maybe former honcho—by the name of Salman Mardam-Bey?"

A LOOK AT: THE FIRES OF ALLAH
(CODY'S WAR THREE)

FROM THE MODERN MASTER OF THE ACTION ADVENTURE M.I.A. HUNTER SERIES COMES CODY'S MOST DANGEROUS MISSION YET...

Jack Cody is on a healing path, recovering from the personal trauma of loss that left this top American agent with the nickname "Suicide." But Cody's recovery, his personal relationship with his CIA control officer, Sara Durell, and everything else goes on hold when Cody is thrust into his most dangerous mission yet.

Facing off against a deadly axis of evil—American Nazis, Islamic terrorists and stolen Russian nukes—Cody tracks a bullet-splattered trail of deception in a race to stop the destruction of Houston, Texas under a mushroom cloud . . .

"One of the best adventure writers of our time!" - James M. Reasoner, NYT Bestselling author

ABOUT THE AUTHOR

Stephen Mertz is an American fiction author who is best known for his mainstream thrillers and novels of suspense. His work covers a wide variety of styles from paranormal dark suspense (Night Wind and Devil Creek) to historical speculative thrillers (Blood Red Sun) and hardboiled noir (Fade to Tomorrow). Mertz is also a popular lecturer on the craft of writing and has appeared as a guest speaker before writer's groups and at universities.

Steve's writing output increased dramatically when he emerged as one of the country's most in-demand writers of adventure paperback novels, averaging four books per year for ten years. His work on Don Pendleton's Mack Bolan series is regarded by fans as some of the best in that series. He also created the Mark Stone: MIA Hunter and Cody's Army series, written under the pseudonyms Jack Buchanan and Jim Case respectively.

Stephen Mertz lives in the American Southwest, and he is always at work on a new book.

Find Stephen online: www.stephenmertz.com